The Olive Tree

by Cheryl Thomas

PublishAmerica
Baltimore

First printing

ISBN: 1-4137-6603-X
PUBLISHED BY PUBLISHAMERICA, LLLP
www.publishamerica.com
Baltimore

Printed in the United States of America

The Olive Tree

To Barb & Jim –
I will always
remember Mt. Sinai!

Cheryl

Romans 10:1

Chapter 1

The old man stood, bent and frail, his hands folded on the ship's rail in front of him. A light breeze tousled the few remaining strands of white hair around his wrinkled and weary face. The sun beat down mercilessly, yet went unnoticed by the old man as the worn creases around his mouth moved rhythmically.

A boy waited patiently nearby, copying the pose of the man beside him. He thought himself nearly a man now. He would be 13 years old in just under a year. Of course that was the reason for this trip, wasn't it? His parents had told him little except that he would be going to Jerusalem with this old man to study. They had called him Gamaliel. "Old man" was just what Saul called him in the privacy of his own thoughts. He had never seen anyone so wrinkled before. And what was that he was doing with his mouth? It looked liked he was talking to himself, but no sound was coming out. Well, maybe he wouldn't be so bad as a teacher. At least he still had his teeth. Saul remembered how his grandfather had looked before his death last year—not quite as wrinkled as the old man standing next to him, but he had had no teeth. He had personally thought that was disgusting. Gums smacking noisily when he ate. The receding chin. How gruesome.

Almost as bad as some of those god-statues that his neighbors had in their house. He could hardly bear even to listen to his grandfather's efforts to speak to him. But then, Saul had felt that nothing he had to say was relevant to him anyway. He was much more interested in talking to men with teeth. And men who could speak Hebrew.

Saul spoke several languages—he had to, living in a commercial city, but he felt that Hebrew was the perfect language—the one that God spoke. That's probably what got him into trouble so much. Saul loved to argue—about anything with anyone. But his favorite arguments had to do with the Hebrew God's superiority. And these men in Tarsus were especially enticing to argue with. So sure of themselves. Happy with the way their lives were. Happy to live day to day, eating, drinking, and partying. The only thing that seemed to upset them was him. Often he would interrupt their merrymaking with a warning of woe or of coming doom. After all, he was learning so much about God's wrath in the daily classes at the synagogue. He just couldn't help himself! Saul was too serious to fit in there. He tried to play and talk with the other boys but they made fun of him. He knew he wasn't the athletic type, but he tried, for goodness sake. If he didn't care for the game, at least he could enjoy the competition.

A sigh escaped unnoticed from Saul's lips. His shoulders hunched over in despair. He felt that he knew the real reason he was on this ship. His parents just couldn't bear to deal with a son who couldn't keep his mouth shut. Everyone in Tarsus complained about him. He had heard his parents whispering about him, caught phrases such as "special problem," "outspoken," "need for more instruction than we can give him," and the one that hurt the most, "send him to Jerusalem." Not take him, just send him. So here he was, with an old man he didn't know, on a ship going far away to Jerusalem. He could almost hear his mother's voice inside his thoughts saying, "Think about the bright side, Saul." So he watched the waves gently nudging the side of the ship and tried and tried to think of the "bright side."

A list slowly formed in his mind. He reached into the folds of his cloak for a scrap of paper he had squirreled away and, with the pen that was always kept behind his ear and the ink kept safely inside the fold of his cloak, he began to write.

"I, Saul, do hereby list the good things about this trip. 1. I am on my own at last. 2. Sarah will be coming to Jerusalem soon to marry and that means 3. My parents will also be along. 4. It will be fun to study all day long and not have to worry about what others think of me."

The elderly gentleman called Gamaliel paused in his prayers and gazed thoughtfully at the frowning young boy beside him. Too young to be so serious, in his opinion. Saul was not like the other boys he had taught these past 30 years. This child would be a challenge. He smiled to himself. "Yes, but a good challenge. At last, someone worthy to pass along all my knowledge to," he thought. "Here is a child who cares about the Scriptures because he believes them, not because he must study them in order to take part in a ceremony or avoid a father's lashing."

It was true. Saul had a black-and-white concept about the world around him. Things were either right or they were wrong. There could be no gray in his existence. He already showed a particularly focused fervor for moral issues and his devotion to the Holy Scriptures was amazing for one so young. The old man reached out and gently laid a gnarled hand on Saul's shoulder.

"You remind me of myself, Saul, when I was your age."

Saul smiled in reply, and for a brief moment his features were lit in pleasure. "Well, at least you must like me, then."

Gamaliel chuckled. "Yes, son, I do like you very much, although I have seen how hard it is to get along with you. Your parents are very frustrated with you, and your sister Sarah, well, I think that if it were not for the fact that she has her mind on her wedding, she would probably be plotting a way to leave you in a ditch like Joseph's brothers did."

Saul's frown returned and he quickly glanced away. "I...I always try to be respectful...but there are certain things that are wrong and if I don't say anything, well, then I am just as wrong as they are! You should know that, sir. I understand you are a great teacher of the Scriptures. My father says you are the most knowledgeable teacher since Moses."

Gamaliel smiled. "The study of the Scriptures has been my life's work since I was able to toddle around after my father and ask questions. Yet I have not mastered it all. There are many things in Scripture I still do not fully comprehend."

"Please go on. I would like to hear more," Saul prodded. Could it be possible that this ancient man might have more to learn about God? Surely if he studied so hard during his whole lifetime he would know all there was to know.

"Are you so ready to get on with your studies?" Gamaliel asked. Saul nodded, his attention focused on the old man's piercing eyes.

"Well, then, here is your first question. Perhaps we can figure it out together. What does the Scripture say about the coming of Messiah? What kind of person will he be? Where will he come from? What is his mission?"

"Sir, these are the questions you wrestle with?" Saul asked in confusion. "I have studied Isaiah already and am familiar with the references to the Messiah."

"Recite them to me."

Saul's voice rang out with conviction and authority as he began to speak all the passages he could remember. It would be nice to impress this teacher of teachers, so he raised his arms heavenward as he'd seen his father do in the synagogue and began, "A son shall be given to us who will rule for ever and ever. Peace will be established in all the world. He will be of the lineage of David, a branch of the family of Jesse, and will establish his kingdom with justice and righteousness. He will be known as Wonderful Counselor, Mighty God, Everlasting Father, Prince of Peace. He will be empowered by the Spirit of the Lord." He paused slightly, then in the deepest voice he could muster for someone not yet through puberty, "The Lord Almighty will bring this to pass."

Gamaliel tried not to let Saul see him smile in amusement at such theatrical enthusiasm. "Yes, those are a few of the prophecies. We need to work on ordering your thoughts, my son, but I see you have done well in your studies thus far. I am sure even the fish in these dark waters are impressed by your quick recall of such important passages of Scripture. See, they are coming up to see who speaks with such fervor."

Saul laughed. "I guess I got a little carried away."

"Perhaps, Saul. But it is not wrong to care so much about the things of God. You are a true searcher of the Truth."

"I do seek the truth, sir. That is what gets me into trouble." Saul looked boldly up at Gamaliel as he continued. "I know you are a great teacher and a very wise man. But, sir, I must tell you, if I think you are wrong I will say so."

Gamaliel tried hard not to laugh at the awkward-looking boy, standing up as tall and straight as he could, yet reaching only to Gamaliel's bent shoulders, holding his breath as he waited a response to his outburst. Gamaliel did not answer right away. He looked his young pupil over thoughtfully as he inwardly struggled to control his amusement.

Impatient, Saul let out his breath. "Why don't you answer? Did you not hear me? Are you offended? I'm sorry if I offended you. I merely wanted to let you know what you were in for. I truly don't want to cause you trouble. You see, already my mouth has gotten me into trouble and we're not even in Jerusalem yet. I was hoping…" Saul turned his face away, embarrassed to let the old man see how much his opinion meant to him, and angry with himself for once again spoiling everything.

The old man was still silent. He saw the passion, the convictions, the courage in this young boy. Looking through Saul's awkward exterior, Gamaliel saw great strength of character blossoming. This would be a very rewarding year.

"My son," he began patiently, "it is easy to learn the facts and to quote passages. It is not so easy to weave the words and the knowledge into the fibers of your soul. It is the difference between knowing here in your head," Gamaliel placed his hands on Saul's head as if in blessing, then clasped them to his own chest, "and knowing in your heart. You have already begun the journey to the heart. I foresee that you will be a leader in Israel. Perhaps you will be able to bring them back to the God they have forsaken."

Saul was unsure how to answer. He was puzzled by Gamaliel's insistence on a difference between head knowledge and heart knowledge. How could you know something to be true, yet not believe it? Impossible.

"Look, son. There is Caesarea. We will be docking there soon." Gamaliel stretched a long, thin finger toward the approaching shore.

Saul lifted his eyes from the dark water and caught his breath in wonder. "That's quite a city! Look at all the ships! It's a lot like Tarsus, but more, well, organized, I guess." He continued to study the harbor. "Not natural, though. It's man-made."

As they drew closer their ship headed for a gate between two groups of enormous statues. They slid gracefully into the breakwater built by Herod to protect his ships from the currents. Bronzed, well-muscled slaves stood ready to anchor the ropes tossed to them from the ship.

"Ah, yes. Herod's pride and joy. An earthly king with a heart set on earthly treasure." Gamaliel's comment sounded a little different from the instruction Saul was expecting.

"My father told me about this city," Saul continued. "It's very neatly laid out with a very modern and clever water system for bringing in fresh water and flushing away the used, filthy water."

"I wish we could do the same for men's souls as easily, my son." Gamaliel took hold of Saul's arm and walked slowly down the plank toward solid ground.

"You are very similar in many ways to a boy I met quite a few years ago and I have been trying this whole trip to remember his name."

Saul looked at him with interest as they made their way slowly through the crowded dock area. He was amazed at the way most of the people bowed respectfully toward Gamaliel as if he were the emperor himself and how they were careful to let him have the good path and avoid the few mud-filled holes and the piles of donkey manure here and there. It was good to be in such a busy place. It reminded him of home.

"Yeshua! That's it. The boy's name was Yeshua. How could I forget such a name?" Gamaliel seemed eager to talk.

"I'll never forget the day he came to the temple. I was there discussing the Scriptures with some of the other leaders. This boy just walked in and began discussing them with us. He couldn't have been older than twelve—your age. But he knew much more than he should have for one so young. Like you." He smiled at Saul.

"Did he become a student of yours?"

"Oh, no. I think he was just visiting for the Passover. I never did find out who his teacher was, but Yeshua was very well instructed. He spoke as if he knew." Gamaliel paused for a moment, trying to remember. "I don't think it could have been his father. He seemed a simple man, not educated much at all."

"Tell me more about him," Saul begged.

"He was fascinating to listen to. It's not every day such a smart boy comes along! After he had been with us in the temple for quite some time, his father and mother came rushing into the temple, very angry at him for being there."

"Did they not approve of his studies, then?"

"I don't think that was it at all. I overheard them say that they had been on their way home to another town before they realized he was missing and they had searched everywhere for him. The boy seemed surprised that they didn't know where he was." Gamaliel was enjoying the memory.

"You two are very much alike. Both of you enjoy the Scriptures and both of you annoy your parents."

"I would like to meet him!"

"I haven't seen him since that day. He would be about thirty years old or so now, I think. It's strange that I haven't heard more about him. He surely must be a great rabbi somewhere. Unless, of course, he is no longer alive. That would be a pity. He had such great potential. I hope, for Israel's sake, he is alive and well."

Saul had been so engrossed in the conversation that he hadn't noticed how far they had walked. Gamaliel stopped in front of a small house. A stocky, weathered old man came hobbling out to greet them.

"Rabbi Gamaliel! It is good to see you again."

"It is good to see you, too, Rabbi Elioenai."

"Will you be staying long? I hope you will be able to speak in the synagogue this Sabbath. And who is this young man with you?" he cackled. "A new student? What is the news from Jerusalem? Still having trouble with that pesky procurator?" The questions seemed to flow non-stop, one running right into the next. Gamaliel patiently let Elioenai ramble on until he ran out of breath.

Saul stood silently just behind his teacher, not quite as patiently. He shifted from foot to foot. They only had a few hours, after all, before their ship left again and he was anxious to see as much of this city as he could in that time.

"Saul." Gamaliel's voice interrupted his thoughts. "I need to rest a while. Why don't you run to the marketplace and purchase the supplies we need while I visit with my friend?"

"Yes, sir!" Saul tried to keep the grin from spreading too far across his face. He helped Gamaliel into the house then was off, exhilarated with the idea of being by himself, in charge of whatever he felt like doing. This was great. He took a deep breath of city air and took a step toward the market, a step toward independence at last.

Chapter 2

A dark, tousled, curly head peeped around the corner of the house. Her luminous eyes were full of mischief as she placed one small finger over lips that were curved ever so slightly upward. "Sssh!" she whispered to another small figure who had followed her around past the front of the house and into the dim and deserted Jerusalem street.

"But where are we going, Joanna?" a timid voice asked. This child was as different from the first as a raven from a dove. Although her hair was dark, it was braided very neatly and tied with a bow. Her wool gown was freshly washed, her sandals clean and tied around her petite ankles. She looked more the part of a princess than the daughter of a poor potter and his wife. She was their only child and indulged by both of them. The extra attention had only seemed to improve her character rather than spoil her, however. She had, in her seven years of life, never done anything to bring them displeasure. At least, nothing that she could remember. Now, here she was, too early in the morning to even be awake, following Joanna, her very best friend in the whole world, straight into T-R-O-U-B-L-E. She held her breath and raced to catch up to Joanna.

"Wait!" she whispered. "You have to tell me where we're going. My parents will be worried when they find I'm missing. Couldn't we have waited until they woke up to tell them where we would be going? I'm sure that would have been the better way to do this."

"Hush, Abigail!" Joanna clasped a hand over her friend's mouth. Her whole body quivered with the excitement of her secret. "Your parents would never let you go if they knew. That's why we have to get there and back before sunrise. This is too good to miss! I overheard my father and brothers talking last night. They said that a man came into town yesterday and healed that old lame beggar man that sits by our gate. He just walked right up to him and said, 'Be healed' or something like that and the man started jumping all over the place. Come on, let's go see if it's true!"

"I...I...I can't." Abigail turned to leave. She grabbed her friend's hand and pulled her back the way they had come. "Look, it's already getting light."

"Come on, Abigail! Just this once!"

"No. And you have to come home too."

Joanna struggled to free herself from Abigail's terrified grip. "Why? My parents will think I'm off with my sisters gathering wood or something. They'll never miss me."

"But if they do, they'll never let us play together again. Please, Joanna, come home!"

The thought of never playing with Abigail again had its desired effect. Sobered, Joanna turned around with Abigail and slowly trudged off toward home.

"I'm sure we could have gotten away with it." She pouted.

"Well, maybe we can go later, with my father." Abigail tried miserably to console her friend. "Perhaps he'll want to go see this man and we can go too."

Joanna threw her friend a look that said, "No way!" and continued on in silence.

"Well, then, maybe your sisters would take us. Or your brother Matthew."

Joanna's face suddenly brightened. "That's it! Matthew will take us! He'll do anything I say. He's such a pushover. But we'll tell him that we want to go to the market and once we're there we'll just conveniently get lost and he'll find us much later, or perhaps we'll find our own way home after a little side trip...get it?"

"I don't know..."

"Come on! It won't hurt anything. Let's go!"

They had reached Abigail's house and were whispering to each other just outside the door. Abigail's mother poked her head outside and yawned. "Up already, Abigail? Oh, Joanna, hello. What are you two girls up to?"

"Can Abigail come with me to the market? My mother is letting me do the shopping today." The lie rolled easily off of Joanna's tongue.

Abigail's mother studied Joanna's face for a moment. "All by yourself? I find that hard to believe, Joanna."

Joanna's face reddened. "Well, no. That is...uh, Matthew's actually taking me. He has errands to do and my mother said I could go and pick up some oil for her."

Abigail was speechless. She had never heard Joanna lie before. What was happening to her friend? But before she could deny anything, she heard her mother saying, "Well, I guess you are growing up. Go along. Just hurry and be back by noon. Abigail can do her chores then."

"Thanks!" Joanna grabbed Abigail by the hand and hurried in the direction of her own house. Rounding a corner, they almost bumped into Matthew, who was struggling to balance four large clay jars underneath his muscled arms.

"Wow! Slow down, there, little one. Where are you going in such a hurry?"

Joanna stopped to catch her breath. "To find you, Matthew."

Abigail interrupted. "She lied to my mother, Matthew, and said that we were going to market with you this morning. Ouch!"

Joanna had poked her sharply with her elbow.

"Well, now, Joanna. Did you say that? Don't lie to your big brother. You know I can see right through you!" His stern voice was too much for her.

Big tears started to roll down Joanna's cheeks. "I did say that. I just wanted to play with Abigail this morning. We wanted to go see that man that you were talking about and I didn't think we would be allowed to go. I'm sorry."

Matthew put the jars down. "You're right, Joanna. You wouldn't be allowed to go. That's not a sight for a young girl." He knelt down beside her and lifted her chin so that they were eye to eye. "Now, since you said you were going to market with me, you will. And you will both help me carry these jars. Perhaps a mile or so carrying heavy jars will help you to think twice before lying again."

Matthew helped the girls pick up their jars and balance them on their heads, then started off ahead of them toward the marketplace, altering his pace only slightly so that the girls could manage to follow a short distance behind.

Before long they had arrived at the busy marketplace. The noise was almost deafening as merchants from all over the world shouted at potential customers to come and buy. Abigail and Joanna paused to smell the spices from Arabia, then just couldn't pass the Babylonian fabrics without feeling their smooth texture and dreaming out loud of a rich husband who would buy these for them someday. Matthew elbowed his way through the crowd, fighting to get to a cool spot under the only tree in the center of the activity. The girls were slowing him down and he lost the spot to another vendor. Irritated, he took the jars and sent the girls on their way back home.

"Now go straight home. Abigail's mother is expecting her by noon and I will tell her you both lied to her about coming here if you wander off."

Joanna looked as if her adventurous spirit had had enough adventure for weeks. She nodded in obedience. "But, Matthew, do you think it would be all right to take the garden path home? It's so much prettier that way and we won't get into any trouble, I promise!"

He shrugged. "I guess it would be all right. There are some families who came to Jerusalem for the Passover festival who are still camping in the gardens so be polite and don't get in their way. Most should be packing up to leave soon." He turned away from the girls as a well-dressed customer approached and they began pleasantly bartering over the price of the jars.

Joanna and Abigail skipped away unnoticed, hand in hand, and headed toward the city gate behind the temple. The garden just outside the gate was one of their favorite spots and they went there as often as they could to play together and share secrets. They walked hand in hand among the bright red and yellow flowers until they reached a gnarled, old olive tree in the center of the garden. Here they sat, backs against the tree. Abigail slowly twirled a blade of grass as she listened to her friend's chatter.

"Abigail, are you listening?" Joanna turned toward her friend and stared right into her eyes. "You weren't listening!" she scolded. "Now I'll have to start all over again…"

"Look!" Abigail pointed toward the hill in the distance. "I wonder why those women are running."

It was rather unusual to see women running toward the city. Most women took their time when going for water or to the market or on any errands since that was the only time they had time to talk to one another.

"They look strange," Joanna commented. "Perhaps they're being chased by soldiers…no, I don't see anyone else." Joanna stood up and squinted her eyes. "Maybe they're running toward something. Maybe someone is having a baby or something. Let's go see what's happening!" Without waiting for her friend, Joanna dashed off in the direction the women had taken.

"I'm not coming!" Abigail shouted after her. "I have to go home. See you later!" She dusted off her tunic and took one more deep breath of the delicious, sweet-smelling garden air and slowly wandered toward home.

Chapter 3

The sweet garden air was the same. It was so nice to be here again. It seemed an eternity since Saul had been alone in this garden outside Jerusalem. Actually, it had only been six years. Amazing how little things had changed here, at least in the garden. His favorite gnarled olive tree was still standing, a little taller, a little wider than before, but still standing, waiting for him like a true friend.

Unlike Jerusalem. The city had grown in size during his absence. It seemed dirtier and noisier than he remembered from his last Passover visit with his family. Everywhere he went he ran into a donkey or a chicken or worse, stepped over a pile of manure left behind. Even around the temple it was filthy. He wasn't sure which was noisier, the bleating of the lambs or the calls of the merchants selling the animals and exchanging money for sacrifice. Disgusting. Saul took a big breath of the fresh air. This was more like it! He often felt torn between his duties as rabbi and his love for the fresh air and following the trade of his uncle, a tentmaker. He pushed aside a feeling of relief that his temple responsibilities were in Tarsus, not in Jerusalem. It might be blasphemous to be unhappy with God's holy city.

Saul made his way to a large rock in the far corner of the garden. It was surrounded on three sides by ancient olive trees that offered shade from the hot sun. Saul spread his cloak over the rock and sat down. It was so peaceful. There was no one else in the garden, no noise but the songs of birds, the stench of the city replaced by the perfume of brightly colored flowers scattered about. It didn't take long before Saul was lost in thought, mesmerized by the beauty around him.

How he missed Gamaliel. His teacher, his mentor, his friend. His only friend, in fact. At least, at first. Saul smiled as he remembered how Gamaliel had been patient with him, teaching him not only the Holy Scriptures, but also helping to guide his character through the awkward stages of adolescence into manhood, protecting him from himself, in a way. Of the thousands of choices he had made over the years, any one of them could have led him astray, off the path that God had chosen for him. Gamaliel's tutelage had been wise. Saul had learned much about patience and dealing with people from observing the master. He now had a few more friends because of it.

Eyes closed, smiling at the memories, Saul thought of his friend Benjamin. They had studied together with Gamaliel here in Jerusalem for a brief time before Saul returned to Tarsus. Their discussions about the mind of God had been challenging and stimulating. He was an intellectual match for Saul. They had stayed up all night at times, watching the sunset and the sunrise over the same argument. It would be good to see Benjamin again, to be a part of the Sanhedrin with him and be able to discuss Scripture in the same way again.

Saul's eyes flew open. The Sanhedrin! The reason he was here! He glanced at the sun's position. Hopefully he hadn't missed her. His parents had arranged a marriage for him with the daughter of an old family friend and he was supposed to meet her today. Unfortunately he had to be married in order to be a part of the Sanhedrin. Marriage was a bother, in his opinion. He wanted to study, not worry about a wife and children. Although many sons would be nice. Perhaps God would give him sons to discuss the Scriptures with. Now that would be very good.

Gathering his cloak and shaking off the dust and pollen that had fallen on it, Saul raised his hands in benediction. "Thanks be to the God of Creation." And with that, he turned and reluctantly walked back through the garden toward Jerusalem.

The sun had barely peeked over the horizon before Abigail was out of bed, humming softly to herself as she gathered together two sturdy clay pots. As a young woman of sixteen now, she was responsible for getting the day's supply of water from the well and today she was eager to get it done quickly. Normally Abigail would wait for her friends and they would all go together just before sunrise, giggling and gossiping along the way. It was one of the few times they could be together anymore, now that they were "grown-ups" and had more responsibilities at home. It had been quite a while since she and Joanna had run off to tell secrets in their garden or play with the other girls. Abigail balanced one pot on her head, the other on her hip, and walked as quickly as she could toward the well.

Today she couldn't wait for anyone. Today was special. She needed the extra time to bathe and brush her long, silky black hair and dress in her new robe that she'd worked so hard to sew for herself. Today was The Day. Today he would come. Today she would be married.

Setting the pots down, Abigail paused to rest. Shivering slightly in the damp morning air, she was oblivious to the city awakening around her. Instead she was deep in thought, a frown creasing her forehead.

"What if I don't like him?" she thought. "Or worse—what if I absolutely hate him?"

She picked up the pots and continued toward the well, the eagerness gone for the moment.

"But what if I do like him? What if he is so handsome I faint with delight?" She giggled.

A familiar voice broke into her reverie.

"Abigail, how can you be happy at a time like this?"

"Oh, Joanna! You are out early!"

"Of course I am," her friend replied, adjusting the jar on her hip. "I knew you would be here and I just had to see you. How can you be so happy? I would be terrified if I were you, not knowing the man my father was planning to marry me off to!" Joanna brushed back a stray lock of long, curly hair so that Abigail could see her frown of disapproval. She sighed dramatically and, with a real tear making its way down her brown cheek, threw her arms around her best friend. "Oh, Abigail, I will miss you so much!"

"Oh, Joanna!" Abigail set her pots down next to the well. "I still have a few days after the wedding left here in Jerusalem. We won't be leaving for Tarsus until after the next Sabbath. Saul is a rabbi, you know."

Abigail ran her fingers nervously through her hair. In her haste to be up and out this morning she had not taken her usual care to braid it. That would come later. Her mother would help. They had even saved enough money to buy a few jewels and gold strands to weave into the braids for the wedding today.

"It's actually very exciting," Abigail continued. "He is, after all, the protégé of Gamaliel himself. And there are rumors that he will someday be very prominent in the Sanhedrin. He is already listened to with great respect in Tarsus, even by his elders." She leaned in closer to her friend and whispered confidentially, "I am sure I will be the wife of the greatest man in all of Israel."

Joanna giggled. "Oh, Abigail! You've always thought yourself destined to greatness in one way or another. He's a tentmaker, not a king. You will be no better off as his wife than you are now. I wonder how your father ever found such an eligible bachelor!"

Abigail shook her head in annoyance. "My father and his father were boyhood friends. They arranged it long ago. And, anyway, he is certainly more respected here than your betrothed."

Joanna's dark eyes flashed with anger. "Stephen is wonderful."

Abigail's frayed nerves snapped. "He's a goldsmith that makes idols for gentiles! He sells his soul and betrays his people!" Her voice faded as a tear ran down Joanna's cheek.

"Oh, Joanna, I'm sorry!" Abigail was suddenly filled with remorse. "It was mean of me to say those things. Of course Stephen is wonderful! And he does make beautiful jewelry." She paused for a moment, fingering the gold strands in her hair. Her words did not seem to be comforting her friend much.

"Joanna, Stephen is perfect for you. He is the sweetest, gentlest man I have ever known." She gave Joanna a hug. "I'm sorry I said those things. Please forgive me, Joanna. Let's not fight!"

Joanna smiled. "You're right, Abigail. He is very good to me, and everyone else too. My mother is afraid we will be penniless because he's always helping others. I guess that's the only reason he is able to put up with me and my talent for getting into trouble. He pities me and probably thinks he can help me straighten up once we're married."

Abigail giggled. "He's not terribly romantic or exciting, but I think you will find enough excitement for the both of you. You were always good at that! We've had lots of crazy times together, haven't we?"

Joanna shrugged good naturedly. "I can't help it. I'm just lots of fun! Let's go before everyone else wakes up. I want you all to myself this morning."

The girls picked up their pots and began walking slowly toward the well, each lost in her own thoughts. Life was becoming more complex each day. Abigail smiled to herself as she filled her water pots, remembering her simple, carefree days as a child roaming the hills and orchards around Jerusalem. Suddenly, she was seized with a desire to experience that freedom one last time.

"Joanna, I've got to hurry. There's something I must do." Abigail tossed the words over her shoulder as she turned down a side street leading to her house. "I'll see you later."

Abigail hurried as quickly as she could through the narrow, winding streets with the heavy pots of water and left them just inside the door of her house, then ran as fast as her feet would carry her toward her favorite orchard just outside the city gate. Arriving breathless, she closed her eyes in delight at her temporary freedom and sank to her knees under the nearest tree, gasping for air.

"That was quite a race, although I'm afraid you didn't break any records." A deep male voice broke into her thoughts. Slowly she opened her eyes. A man? Talking to her? Here? He must think she was a…no. They were alone, not actually out in public. The garden was very private here.

The face looking back at her was the most striking face she had ever seen. Not handsome, particularly, but memorable. The firm jaw, the full black beard and curly black hair…. She almost reached out to touch it, to run her fingers through the curls, but was paralyzed by his eyes. They were black and piercing. She felt the shock of his gaze as he looked her over from the top of her tousled head with its sparkling beads to the bottom of her dusty feet.

Crimson, she hugged her knees to her chest, still never taking her eyes from his face. She couldn't look away. His eyes held hers, hypnotizing her. And yet she was somehow not afraid. She let her gaze wander down to his full mouth, just beginning to turn up at the corners. She watched in fascination as he spoke, a voice from a dream. Surely that's what this was—a dream.

"Don't be alarmed, little one." He knelt on the ground beside her. "I used to do the same thing as a young boy. My parents brought me to Jerusalem every year at Passover until they were no longer well enough to travel so far." A frown darkened his features for a split second before he continued.

"I used to come to this same orchard seeking refuge from all the hustle and bustle. And I must admit it hasn't lost its charm in all the years I've been away."

Abigail felt the earth begin to spin at his smile. She touched her warm cheeks. "I really must be going. My mother will soon be looking for me. I'm so sorry to have intruded!" She stood awkwardly, brushing away the dirt and dust clinging to her robe. Her eyes met his one last time, longing with all her soul to stay and uncover the mystery of the man within and to touch his face, his hands…. Abruptly, she turned and ran home again, knowing she would never forget him, not daring to wonder at the emotions awakening within her heart.

Chapter 4

Abigail knew from the minute she slipped inside the door of her house that, for the first time in her life, she was in T-R-O-U-B-L-E. She almost giggled, remembering how she had managed to avoid a moment like this with Joanna many times, and now she had done it all by herself.

"Where have you been, child? We have only a few hours to get ready for the wedding! The guests will be arriving soon. Thank goodness Saul's sister offered to help with the food. She is such a sweet girl. I'm so glad she married someone from Jerusalem so we could get to know her." Abigail's mother's anger was forgotten as she continued her chatter, scolding and admonishing her daughter in between bits of village gossip. "Her father and yours were great friends, you know."

Abigail sensed behind her mother's words a sadness too deep for words. "Their lives parallel one another in many ways. They had two children and lost many. We had just you, dear."

"…And lost many more." Abigail silently finished her mother's thought. She saw tears in her mother's eyes and understood. She, too, was leaving. Her husband's home town, Tarsus, was a long way from

Jerusalem, too far to run to her mother for advice or sympathy. And when the children were born...of course there would be children. The thought made her smile. She imagined herself surrounded by healthy, adorable children with beautiful smiles, lovely dark hair and piercing black eyes.

Her hand flew to her mouth in horror. "What am I thinking?" she thought in panic.

At that moment Joanna came through the door, the sparkle in her eyes matching the gold flecks in her new robe, made special for the occasion.

"May I help?" she asked. "I'm ready much too early and it will make the time go by much faster if I could help. My mother said she'd be over in a little while to help too."

"Thank you, Joanna," Abigail's mother answered in relief. "There is so much left to do before the wedding can begin. And I am having trouble braiding Abigail's hair." She held up hands bent and twisted with age. "These just don't work like they used to. Why don't you see what you can do with it."

Joanna took the brush from her calloused hands and began the task of unknotting Abigail's thick hair.

"Where have you been and what have you been doing to get your hair tangled so?"

Abigail put a finger to her lips and waited until her mother left the house before answering.

"Oh, Joanna, you'll never believe it! I think I saw an angel."

Joanna wasn't sure if Abigail was teasing or perhaps delirious from the heat and all the excitement.

"What are you talking about?"

"After I left you this morning I ran to the gardens where we used to play. Out of thin air a gorgeous man appeared. At least, he looked like a man but his eyes were, well, special."

"How?" Joanna was clearly skeptical. Her friend was crazy. Absolutely insane. It must be this wedding to a stranger that had done it to her. Maybe she could come live with her and her new husband Stephen and no one would have to know.

"I don't know how to explain it. They were just very intense."

"Did he give you a message from God?" Joanna asked quietly. Maybe if she just played along for a while....

Abigail thought for a moment. "No. He just mentioned something about his parents bringing him to Jerusalem every year at Passover and that he used to hide in the garden."

Joanna stopped brushing and took Abigail's face in her hands.

"Abigail, angels don't have parents, don't need to hide in gardens, and always bring a message from God."

Abigail looked crestfallen. "I was so sure he was an angel because there was something so unique about him." She continued as if remembering a dream.

"Our eyes met and I felt like I would drown in them. I felt so helpless, yet drawn to him. I wanted to touch him, to caress his face, to hold his hand..." She snapped back to the present. "See! He has some kind of power. If he wasn't an angel, who do you suppose he was?"

Abigail glanced up at Joanna, who was standing very still, her face ashen, the brush frozen in mid-air.

"Joanna, what is it? You're scaring me!"

"Abigail, I know those feelings. I have those feelings—about Stephen—because I love him. But you—you are going to marry Saul today. You shouldn't be having those feelings about another man."

"No! It's impossible! It's not the same."

"You said you wanted to touch him. In what way? Like petting a donkey or..." Abigail tried to avoid her friend's accusing look. "Like caressing a husband?"

Abigail couldn't answer. She feebly waved one hand as if to dismiss such an impossible idea.

"What else did you look at besides his eyes? His mouth? Tell me! Did you wonder what it would be like to kiss him? Abigail, don't lie to me! I'm your friend, your best friend!"

Tears slid easily down Abigail's cheeks as she realized the truth. "What am I going to do? I don't even know who he is."

Joanna resumed the braiding, determined to help her friend. "What can you do? You have to marry Saul or disgrace your father.

Let's not dwell on it. Think about something else. Tell me how your father chose Saul for you." As her mouth spoke the words, her mind was busy scheming. After all, wasn't she a master schemer? Hadn't she always come up with great ideas to get them out of trouble?

Abigail sighed, trying to stop her tears. "I don't dare ever think of him again, do I? Well, maybe I'll feel the same way about Saul—someday." But the tears wouldn't stop. "Oh, Joanna, it's no use!"

"Hush! Dry your eyes quickly. Your mother's coming! We can't let her find out about this. Now, tell me about Saul."

Abigail mopped at her eyes with a corner of her veil. "Well, I don't know too much about him, except that he is a rabbi…"

"And will someday be the greatest in the Sanhedrin!" Joanna joined in the last phrase with Abigail, word for word. Abigail giggled and Joanna sighed with relief. The crisis had passed—for now.

"You know, Joanna, I just don't understand God." Abigail shook her head. "I wonder if I'll be a good wife for a rabbi."

"Of course you don't understand God, Abigail. No one can understand him."

"But why not? Doesn't he want us to understand him? Someday I will find the answers!"

Joanna laughed. "You are full of surprises today, Abigail. One minute crying over a man you don't know and the next trying to figure out the almighty God. It's a good thing you are marrying a rabbi. Perhaps he can answer your questions! Why haven't you two met before if your fathers were such good friends?"

"I guess because Saul's family moved to Tarsus before he was born and we've stayed in Jerusalem. Saul was here for a little while to finish his studies, but then he went back to Tarsus. Our fathers have written to each other over the years, though. I guess that's how they arranged the wedding. It's sad, really."

"Why?" Joanna was sorry she asked that as soon as it was out of her mouth. Anything sad might start those tears flowing again and she was sure she would get blamed if Abigail's mother came back and saw her daughter crying hysterically.

"Maybe we should talk about something happy today, Abigail."

"It's sad because they were such good friends, like we are, but they lived in different parts of the world, just like we will! Promise me we'll stay friends no matter what!" Abigail threw her arms around Joanna and the two girls embraced for a moment.

"Of course we will! I could never forget you!" Joanna comforted them both. "Maybe Saul will bring you to Jerusalem each year for the Passover and we'll see each other then. It's nice that Saul was agreeable to the marriage arrangement, not having met you before. "

"Well, we have met, but I don't remember him at all. His parents used to come as often as they could to Jerusalem at Passover time. His father was never really strong, you know. I stayed out of the way mostly. They were very strict Jews and the boys weren't allowed to play much. Just study all the time."

"How awful!" Joanna's nose wrinkled in distaste.

"Not really. I think it might have been fun to study. At least they didn't have to do chores!"

The girls giggled as Joanna put the finishing touches on Abigail's hair. Abigail pulled the new linen gown carefully over her head.

"Oh! This is beautiful!" Joanna's voice was tinged with jealousy. "The embroidery is perfect! Not one loose stitch!"

Abigail smiled as she smoothed the creases on the gown. "I've been working on it every evening by lamplight after everyone is asleep. Not even my mother has seen it yet!" She tucked a few of the stray blue and yellow threads into the weave of the white linen.

Faint strains of music reached their ears and the voices of excited guests could be heard coming closer. Abigail jumped up from the bench and clung to her friend.

"I can't do this," she whispered, panicking.

"You have to!"

"But what if I don't like him? What if he takes me to Tarsus and I never see you again? What if...."

Joanna pulled away, wrapped the wedding mantle around Abigail, and gave her a little push toward the door. This was one problem she couldn't find a way out of now. It was too late. She choked back a sob.

"Go," she said, wiping a tear from her own eyes. "Your bridegroom is coming."

There was dust swirling everywhere and noise and confusion and music and laughing. Abigail was herded by friendly hands in the direction of her bridegroom. He was coming down the street toward her, surrounded by a crowd of people. They all looked so happy, singing and shouting along the way. She wanted to shout, "Stop! Stop!" but couldn't open her mouth. It was all happening so fast and then—silence.

Although the sounds had not diminished around her she heard nothing but a great empty, echoing silence. There before her stood a crowd of people who, one by one, as if in slow motion, melted away, leaving her standing alone to face Saul of Tarsus, her bridegroom. This was it. She shut her eyes tightly, wishing it was all a dream, praying it was not real. Not today. Not now that she'd met someone that stirred her heart like no other.

Abigail felt a touch on her hand and knew instinctively that it was his touch, his hands taking her hands in his, leading her. She heard the drone of the rabbi and yet still kept her eyes squeezed tightly shut. One moment blended into the next as her mind shut out the reality of what was happening around her. She felt dizzy, faint. Then, those hands again, taking hers. She began to relax in the strength of those hands, imagining that they were the garden man's hands. In her mind she saw him again and her heart cried out for... what? She didn't know. Perhaps whatever it was she would find with Saul. Slowly, slowly she opened her eyes, her lashes thick with unshed tears, and found herself looking into piercing black eyes, holding hers with hypnotic fascination.

Was she dreaming? Had God spared her from reality? Or had he granted her a reality far better than her dreams?

"There's no need to run this time, Abigail, my wife."

All the emotions Abigail had experienced earlier that day came flooding back. She felt her cheeks flush hot with delight.

"I didn't know who you were in the garden."

His smile was teasing her now. "And if you had? Would you still have run from me?"

Saul's eyes roamed appreciatively over his new bride. Surely God had been good. He had needed a wife and would have been willing to take one regardless of her appearance, but this girl was beyond anything he had ever imagined. He recalled her flowing dark hair, now braided and wound around her head, framing the most beautiful face he had ever seen! Large eyes gazed trustingly into his, so innocent, so full of untouched and unexplored emotion. Her cheeks were flushed a faint pink from excitement and her skin was so flawless she appeared to have stepped out of Heaven itself.

"Are you pleased with me, then?" Abigail's halting and breathless words broke into his thoughts just in time.

"I must not get too attached," Saul reminded himself inwardly. He had no desire to fall in love. Only marry and procreate in order to be a part of the great Sanhedrin. Nothing must stand in the way of his pursuit of truth. Not even his new, and beautiful, wife.

Chapter 5

It was wonderful! Abigail hummed to herself and danced around the room as she swept. Marriage was even better than she had imagined. Now she had status as a wife and potential child-bearer. Of course, it had only been five days since her wedding but she prayed every chance she got that God would bless their union with a child, a son. Then, she was sure, Saul would love her as much as she loved him. Tomorrow they would begin their journey to Tarsus and there would not be privacy enough on the ship to indulge in lovemaking. Tonight might be her last chance to conceive that son. She put away the broom and once more stirred the pot of soup cooking over the fire. She added a little wine for seasoning. Tonight must be perfect. She smoothed her hair as she heard Saul's footsteps approaching on the road outside.

Saul came in, hungry for the savory food he had smelled from a few houses away. Abigail hoped he liked having a wife. It was sometimes hard to tell from the way he treated her. She tried her best to keep the house spotless, cook delicious meals, and never get in his way. A perfect wife. Yet Saul was distant, a stranger still. At least he never beat her like she had seen some husbands do to their wives.

Abigail let her fingers brush against his rough, strong hands as she ladled out the soup into his bowl and handed it to him. She tried not to blush as his dark eyes lingered on her bosom as she bent over to give him some bread. At least that was one part of their relationship that satisfied both of them.

"How was your day?" Abigail broke the silence tentatively.

"Fine."

"Did you discuss great things with your friends here?"

"Of course. More bread, please."

Abigail sighed and broke off another piece of bread. Stick to simple topics. "Is the soup to your liking? Shall I get you some more wine?"

"Mmm. Thanks."

Abigail poured the wine and sat quietly, studying her husband. He was so smart. He knew so many things. She wished she dared voice some of her questions. Surely Saul would know the answers. When he had finished eating, she cleared away the dishes, then came and sat at his feet.

"Saul…" Abigail placed her hand tenderly on Saul's arm. "Would you tell me some of the things that you talk about with your friends?" He smiled at her and she was encouraged to continue. "Tell me about God, for instance. Why has he been silent for so many years? Where are the prophets? Have we been forgotten?"

"I sometimes forget that you are still a child in so many ways—so curious about things that needn't concern you." He pulled her onto his lap and nibbled playfully at her neck. "Yet how can one blame me when you have the body of such a beautiful woman."

Abigail wiggled out of his embrace. "I am not a child. I am your wife and I will grant you one desire for every question that you answer," she teased.

Saul grinned and leaned back on his couch, his hands behind his head. "OK, temptress. I will answer one question. Has God forgotten us? No. There, that was an answer. Now come here." He reached for Abigail. She giggled and ran to the opposite side of the room.

"That wasn't a real answer! You must explain a yes or a no."

"That wasn't in the rules!" Saul argued, enjoying their game. He stood up and Abigail screeched in mock fear as he took a step in her direction.

"Saul!"

"OK, wife. I will indulge you." Saul sat back down. "No, God has not forgotten us. I believe he is biding his time, waiting for just the right moment and then the Messiah will come. Perhaps there will be more prophets, perhaps not. Who can know the mind of God?"

Saul forgot for a moment that he was speaking to a mere woman, and spoke to Abigail as a friend.

"I feel inside that the time will be soon. The time is ripe for some kind of divine intervention. The Romans have forced us to live under their rule. We cry out as a people for rescue, just as our nation did as slaves in Egypt long ago. At that time God sent a man named Moses to rescue Israel. I do not know who he will send this time. Perhaps I will be involved."

Abigail was trying to make sense of his answer. "Do you mean you will fight the Romans? Oh, Saul! Stay with me. Don't go!" She threw herself into Saul's arms.

He laughed. "You see why I don't discuss these things with you? You don't understand the whole picture. You see only how it will affect your life. I must be willing to do whatever God asks me to do." He held her to him and stroked her hair absentmindedly. "I have only one goal—to serve my God. Nothing must stand in the way." His hands stopped their movement and he rested a cheek on the top of her head. "Not even you," he whispered silently to himself. "I must remember that."

Abigail gazed invitingly into his eyes. "Thank you for answering my question. Now, husband, what is your desire?"

In answer, Saul pulled her close and kissed her passionately, trying to remember something important. Something he was never to let happen. Instead, he let go of his lingering misgivings and gave in to his emotions. This time, Abigail felt his passion was different. This time, he loved her.

Chapter 6

He was a man possessed, relentlessly pacing from one corner of the room to the other, his hands clenched at his sides in smoldering anger.

"Gamaliel is wrong! He must be wrong about this man. It is impossible!"

Abigail crouched in another corner of the room, bent over the letter from her husband's mentor. It had arrived moments ago. She had asked Saul to read it to her but instead he had flung it onto the floor. Never had she seen Saul so agitated. And today of all days she wanted his attention. She hoped her news would bring a better reaction than Gamaliel's news had.

"Please, Saul, read the letter to me. Perhaps his meaning will be clearer read aloud, or perhaps there is something there that you missed. Please!"

Abruptly Saul stopped pacing and grabbed the letter from her outstretched hands. Seeing the terror on her face, he immediately softened and gathered her into his arms. "I'm sorry, Abigail. I didn't mean to frighten you. But this is tragic news! Come." He led her out onto the roof of their modest home, secluded from the worst of the city, and central to the Jewish community in Tarsus. They sat together in the bright sunshine as Saul spread out the parchment. Abigail could make out only a few words, like Jerusalem and Yeshua. She pointed to the last one.

"Yeshua. I know that name from somewhere."

Saul spit. "Blasphemer! He was crucified for his sins."

Abigail gently touched Saul's arm. "Please read me the letter."

Saul was about to refuse, but how could he deny her anything? Her soft voice, her magical touch, her silky hair, her gentle spirit had ensnared him completely. At first he had resisted the feelings, afraid they would get in the way of his goal. He had tried to think about her as just a necessary part of The Plan. But it had been hopeless. Day by day he had fallen more and more in love with this amazing girl, no, woman now. He smiled, remembering their wedding night only six months ago. She had come to him as innocently as a child, yet as shapely and willingly as a woman in love. He knew she had loved him even then. It was a new experience for him to be loved so completely. Yes, he was admired by many who saw in him a sincerity of heart and purpose. But only Abigail had seen his secret faults and still loved him. She had listened to embarrassing stories of his childhood and not laughed. Instead she had gently stroked his hair and kissed him with her sweet mouth, feeling his pain. She had not once complained about being in Tarsus, although he knew she must miss her family in Jerusalem very much. Could there be a more perfect woman?

"Saul. What's wrong? You're staring at me." Abigail wondered if he knew. Had he guessed what she needed to tell him today?

Saul pulled her close and kissed her gently. "I'm just thinking how wise our fathers were to arrange this marriage for us. I can't ever imagine a life without you."

"Nor I without you, dear husband. Now what could be so awful in that letter to upset our bit of heaven on earth?"

Saul's face darkened once again, although he held his temper in check.

"Here, I will read it to you." He smoothed out the parchment.

"'My dear Saul, You have been like a son to me in these last days I have left here on earth. I felt I could not rest in Abraham's bosom without telling you what has been often on my heart and always in my mind these last few months. After I returned to Jerusalem I heard fantastic stories about a man called Yeshua, born in Bethlehem and raised in Nazareth, who healed the sick, cast out demons, and even brought dead people back to life. Quite a few people here claim he is the Messiah. At first I assumed it was merely the ravings of a few of our people who were desperate for escape from the Romans who torment us here in Jerusalem. At the insistence of my friends in the Sanhedrin, this man was captured and crucified, although they kept that part of the story very quiet. I assumed they had acted wisely and went about my business after returning to Jerusalem. Even after I returned, events were unsettled. Many here claimed this Yeshua was dead only three days, then rose from the dead, alive and well. Not only that, but he went up in the clouds and disappeared, saying that he would come back and take those who believed in him to the very place he was then going. Ludicrous! Totally insane! But, Saul, as I listened to those stories and went back to the Scriptures about the Messiah it seems possible that there may be something to all of this. I am too old and feeble to write all I have learned, and I dare not entrust these thoughts to any but you. I urge you to study for yourself, to see if this Yeshua was—and is—our Messiah.'"

Saul leapt to his feet and tore the parchment into tiny pieces. "No more! I will not listen to this! Senility! It has to be that! Gamaliel was too wise in his younger days to listen to such stories as this. This is blasphemy! Unforgivable…eternal death…I will pray for his soul. No! Oh, no!" He collapsed, his fury barely suppressed as he buried his head in Abigail's lap. She cradled his trembling body until he rested, emotionally exhausted. Not even the death of his parents had caused such pain. They had not turned their backs on the True God. He reached out to his wife for the comfort of her touch with an abandoned desire, for a while escaping his tortured thoughts by losing himself in the silkiness of her body.

Passions spent, they lay together, listening to the sounds of the night creeping in around them…the peeping of toads, the chirping of crickets, the bleating of the sheep on the hillside. In the solace of

Abigail's embrace, the world did not seem so topsy-turvy after all. Perhaps he had read too much into the letter. It may have been another of the Great Teacher's ways of igniting his desire to learn and study more and more. Of course! Many times Gamaliel had taken the wrong side of an issue to get Saul to think things through and not merely rely on rote knowledge.

Saul stroked Abigail's hair and smiled in relief. She noticed the change in mood and kissed his chin playfully.

"You are feeling better now?"

"Yes. Gamaliel must be trying to get me to research this question so that I would be ready to answer any false teacher that dares to stir up our people. Any rabbi worthy of the Sanhedrin must be prepared to refute these kinds of rumors with sound scripture. I will be ready. I will study." He kissed the top of Abigail's head and tossed off her covering. "Tomorrow."

Abigail giggled and pulled her robe around her. "Saul, there is something I want to tell you first."

"Can't it wait until morning?" He kissed the back of her neck.

"Well, actually, it probably could wait until after the Feast of Tabernacles, but I doubt much later than that. I think that five more months are about all it will wait." Abigail took one of Saul's wandering hands and laid it gently on her belly.

The kisses stopped abruptly. Saul looked at where she had placed his hand, then into her smiling eyes.

"You mean…"

Abigail nodded. "I'm sure now."

Saul leapt to his feet, dancing around and around the room, elated. Finally, a child!

Abigail laughingly tossed him his clothes. "You'd better put these on before the neighbors come to see what you are making so much noise about." Abigail's happiness was complete. A wonderful husband and now a child.

"A child! At last we are going to have a child!"

Saul ran out the door, anxious to tell his friends the good news. He murmured excitedly to himself as he went, "My goal is almost complete. A wife. And now a child on the way. Soon I will be a part of the Sanhedrin!"

Abigail hugged her knees to her chin and finished his thought in her own way. "And we can go back to Jerusalem. Home."

Chapter 7

The trip back to Jerusalem was long. Saul paced back and forth on the deck of the ship, hands clasped behind his back, a frown creasing his forehead. It was Abigail's turn to watch her husband's mouth move with no sound. Praying again, no doubt. She could only guess what he was thinking since he had not spoken to her at all since they had boarded the ship a week ago. Whenever she attempted to speak to him or touch him, Saul had closed his eyes and waved her away with a flick of his hand. The strong hand that had always been so gentle was now frightening in its dismissal of her. She didn't understand.

Saul disappeared into the hold below. Abigail couldn't bring herself to move. A pout formed on her lips. Alone on the deck now, she tossed back her head covering and felt the breeze of the cool night air on the strands of hair that tumbled, loosed from the bands that usually held them so neatly. If this was how her husband was going to be then she couldn't wait to get back to Jerusalem and be with her family. She hadn't realized until now just how much she missed them all. She had been too wrapped up in Saul—or her romantic vision of him—to think about much else.

Saul's family had been nice to her, though. His mother had been happy to have an extra pair of hands to help with the work and his father had treated her like a special daughter. It was almost like marrying into royalty. The people of Tarsus had certainly bowed to Saul's father as if he were a king. She had loved listening to the stories he told about how he and her father had been boys together in Jerusalem and how he had become a wealthy and successful merchant yet had remained friends with her father, a poor potter. Her father was a Jew, despised by the Romans, while Saul's father, also a Jew, had become a Roman citizen by order of the emperor. Abigail wasn't sure how much of the story was truth and how much he had embellished over the years. He told her that many years ago he was in Rome and had sought an audience with the emperor in order to sell some imported carpets. The emperor was snacking on grapes as he listened to the sales pitch and had suddenly choked. Saul's father reached in and pulled out the grape, saving the life of the emperor. The emperor had been so grateful that he had decreed this to be a great act of loyalty to Rome and granted citizenship to this Jewish merchant from Tarsus. And he had bought all the carpets, making Saul's father a very wealthy man.

Abigail smiled, remembering the enthusiasm of the storyteller and the way his wife had clicked her tongue and thrown up her hands. Yes, life was good. She had to admit that it was extremely nice to be wealthy. She had gotten used to that very fast. Spoiled, even. Her mother-in-law had taken her often to the marketplace and given her free reign with the servants. Abigail had been able to choose fabrics from her father-in-law's inventory to make new tunics for her expanding figure. And it was her father-in-law's money that had made it possible for her and Saul to go back to Jerusalem. He had sent a great deal of it to the Sanhedrin to open up the way for Saul to become a member there.

So far in life, Saul had accomplished everything he set out to do. First, schooling with Gamaliel, the most respected rabbi in Israel. Then, becoming a rabbi himself. A Pharisee among Pharisees. Next, a Jewish wife and children. Abigail rubbed her swollen belly with the palm of her hands. And finally, a member of the Sanhedrin. She was proud of Saul and could hardly wait to see Joanna again to boast about her husband! Perhaps he was thinking through his next goal and that was why he had ignored her lately. She would be patient. Anyway, there would be a little one to occupy her time soon—and he would be just as perfect as her husband. Two gods instead of one, all her very own.

Abigail leaned over the side of the boat and felt a trickle of liquid on her legs. Startled, she stepped back away from the railing. There was more now, pouring from somewhere within her. Frightened, she looked down at her soaked gown and knew that this was something more than the accidents she used to have as a toddler. She felt a tightening around her belly and thought the hand of God was squeezing the life from her. She stumbled to the women's deck below and lay in a crumpled heap in the farthest corner she could find. She was alone and scared. What was happening? She hadn't really meant that about Saul being a god. She thought that perhaps the One True God had heard her and was punishing her for the blasphemous thought. Saul had told her that He did things like that.

Oh, the pain! It gripped her again and again without mercy. She slipped in and out of consciousness through the night, only faintly aware of the blood soaking the floor around her. In between the pain she called out for help, her voice barely a whisper. There were bright lights floating around her and, in her hallucinations, seemed to come right through the walls. The lights had hands that felt cool to her fevered head and kind faces that seemed to comfort her through the night.

"Abigail! Abigail!" A man's voice penetrated the cloudiness of her mind. She heard women's voices too, far away, saying, "Poor girl. Her baby must be cursed. We saw the feet first. Very unusual. Very bad omen." Then the man's voice. "Stop the chatter and help me. Go get cloths—lots of them. Now!" The women scampered away to do his bidding, clicking their tongues in disapproval.

"Now is the time for your Jewish God to help." Abigail heard the voice just as she felt the innermost part of her body being torn in two.

Her screams echoed in her head and she reached desperately for the hand of one of the bright ones. But they were gone.

Abigail opened her eyes and saw a baby being lifted from between her naked legs. It was a boy baby, its misshapen head and bluish-grey color grotesque. She had only time to wonder about its silence before the vomit came and she drifted into unconsciousness again.

Chapter 8

The pain was gone. Abigail opened her eyes. She felt the gentle motion of the boat rocking in still waters and the sound of wood bumping wood. They must have docked during the night.

"There, there, just rest, you poor girl," a soothing mother-voice crooned softly beside her.

Abigail did feel weak. And thirsty. "I...water..." she managed to croak through parched lips.

"Of course, dear. Here you are." The woman gently lifted Abigail's head and helped her drink a little wine from a new goatskin pitcher. "That Greek doctor says you should have as much wine as you wish. The other women and I thought you would never make it through the night, but that doctor had the hands of a god. A real miracle, it was, saving your life!"

Abigail's eyes filled with tears. She rested both hands on her belly. "My baby...is dead?"

The other woman was silent for a moment. "No. Not dead. One of the other women took him to hold him through the night and keep him warm. A small one, he is. Lucky for you he was small, I guess, since he was born upside down. You lost a lot of blood as it was." She paused for a moment, then continued in warning. "A bad omen, for sure. It's known in my country that a child born upside down is cursed by the gods. Pity on his poor parents! We should have let him die. It would have been kinder to you, I think."

Abigail heard only that her child was not dead and began to cry harder. "A boy! A son for Saul! Oh, where is he now? Please bring him to me!" She hung desperately to the woman's cloak.

"Did you not hear what I'm telling you? The child is a curse. Perhaps if we threw him overboard as a sacrifice to the gods, then we could save you and your husband from the evil. The child is sickly and probably won't survive anyway."

"No!" Abigail gasped in horror. "Never!" She struggled to her feet. "I must find him. I must…" She collapsed to her knees, too weak to stand. "He's my baby. You can't have him. Saul! Oh, Saul, my husband…" Abigail crawled as far as she could, pushing her frail body to its limits in her desperation.

A shadow crossed the doorway. "What's this?"

Abigail remembered the booming voice from her semiconscious state last night.

"Why is my patient crawling across the floor?" He pointed an accusing finger at the woman. "You were told to watch her and call me as soon as she woke. Help me carry her back to her bed."

His voice sounded stern, but Abigail's desperation gave her courage. "Where is my son? Why have you taken him from me? Please don't throw him in the water. Who are you? Where is my husband Saul? We don't believe in your gods. Our God would never ask such a sacrifice. Please!" Abigail's body shook with her sobs as she pleaded for the life of her son.

"First things first." The man's voice was now soft as he addressed her. "I am a physician. My name is Luke. Your God helped me save you and your son last night. Therefore, you do not need to fear that I would have anything to do with destroying a life that your God wished to be saved. I have seen his power many times in my profession and, although I am Greek, I have become a believer in the One True God and am on my way to Jerusalem to learn more about him. Your husband has offered to instruct me as payment for my services so we will be continuing this journey together on foot as soon as you are strong enough. Saul has gone ashore to purchase supplies."

"Sir," Abigail hesitated slightly, "my son...where is he?"

"Hannah!" Luke's voice echoed effortlessly throughout the ship. "Bring the child!" In a softer voice he explained, "My wife has watched him through the night for you. Ah, Hannah. This is the child's mother. I will leave you to attend her. That slave woman was worthless. See, she is gone already, probably hiding in some corner." With that, he left the two women together.

Abigail gingerly sat up and shyly held out her arms toward the plump matron who cradled her baby. "May I hold him?"

"Of course." Hannah tenderly laid the child near Abigail's bosom. He began to suck noisily and Abigail laughed for the first time in many weeks. She stroked his head and kissed his fingers one by one. His tiny hand grabbed her finger and held on tightly as he nursed hungrily.

"Abigail, there are a few things you should know." Hannah was reserved.

"Oh, Hannah, thank you so much for taking care of him for me. Just seeing him makes me feel so much better! I feel as if I could fly to Jerusalem! Isn't he just perfect?"

"Abigail, please listen." Hannah's plump face magnified the creases above her forehead. "I've assisted in the births of many babies yet have never seen a birth as difficult as this one. You will recover, praise God, but your son, well, he may be different from the other boys, if he survives at all."

"Different? Of course! He is special. The answer to my husband's prayers. He will be a great rabbi like his father." Abigail nestled his sleeping head on her shoulder.

Hannah continued as gently as she could. "It took too many minutes for this child to begin breathing after birth. To me, he appeared stillborn, but my husband prayed to the One True God and rubbed his arms and legs and he gasped one or two times then began breathing. Off and on through the night we experienced the same thing. Breathing, not breathing. Shaking violently, then still. Almost like he couldn't make up his mind whether he wanted to stay with us or go off to heaven."

Abigail hugged her son. "He needs me."

"And his head, Abigail. It's not quite right. It doesn't look like…"

"He's perfect, just perfect," Abigail cut her off with a sob.

Hannah bent over the young girl and gave her a motherly kiss on the top of her head. "Yes, he is, Abigail." She sighed. "Perhaps too perfect for this world. You rest now. He can sleep beside you for a while." She tucked in the cloak around Abigail and her baby. "I'll stay and keep watch."

"Thank you, Hannah." Abigail yawned. Her eyes closed and she drifted off to sleep, comforted again in her drowsiness by those bright beings hovering near her son.

Chapter 9

For seven days Abigail lay in a dark room of the house of an absent merchant friend of Saul's in the city where the servants had carried her. Saul did not come see her once during that time. She was ceremonially unclean and knew that he would follow the law to the letter. She was glad for the rest anyway and Hannah had been great company. They had chatted for hours like old friends.

Hannah had become a surrogate mother to Abigail and taught her how to take care of her new baby. Abigail hadn't had any younger brothers or sisters to practice mothering so she didn't know to worry that her baby was so quiet and his cry so weak. And Hannah didn't have the heart to discourage her. Mostly his seizures came when Abigail was sleeping and it was Hannah who held and rocked the infant through most of the night, encouraging him to breathe when his little body grew still. Night after night she prayed to the God of Israel to spare the life of this precious little one. But she was afraid. Afraid for the little boy and for his unsuspecting young mother. Afraid that when the father saw the boy he would know there was something terribly wrong and would blame the mother.

She had been observing Saul from afar and had been able to pry some information about him from her husband. He was a perfect man as far as she could tell: careful to obey every single part of the law, praying often to his God, studying the Holy Scriptures from dawn till dusk, minding his own business, never a bad word from his mouth. No, there would be nothing in his life to blame for a child such as this. But then, there was little in Abigail's life to blame either. From what Abigail had told her, she had been an obedient child and a dutiful and loving wife. Hannah shook her head in exasperation. Let the tongues in Jerusalem wag all they wanted to, she was not going to blame either of them. And maybe, just maybe, God would perform another of those miracles she had heard about. She had heard that there had been a man who had healed children worse off than this little one. Come to think of it, it was the same group of men that Saul wanted to be a part of that had killed the healer prophet! If Saul had already been a part of the Sanhedrin he might have been able to convince the others to spare this man's life. Too bad how some things work out in life.

Hannah yawned and gently shook Abigail awake. It had been a long night but the child had made it through once again. Perhaps things wouldn't be so bad after all.

"Day eight, Abigail. The sun is almost up. Take your son for a while. I think he is hungry and I need to sleep for a little while before the moyel arrives for the ceremony today."

"You spoil him, Hannah, by holding him through the night. What will I do when we no longer have you around?" Abigail took the baby and put him to her breast. His eyes flickered opened for a moment, then closed again.

"See, he isn't hungry yet. I can sleep a few more minutes."

"No, Abigail. He hasn't eaten all night and needs to nurse now. You must try to get him to take the breast even if he doesn't seem hungry. He doesn't know yet what is good for him."

"Oh, all right. Come here, little one." Abigail turned his face toward her and brushed her nipple near his mouth. "Eat now. No, not that way, here. You must eat if you want to grow up strong like Abba. Today you will see him and he will choose a name for you. I wonder what name Saul will choose. Have you heard any clues from your husband about a name for our little one?" She glanced in Hannah's direction and saw that she had already fallen asleep on her mat, which she had placed only a few feet away. Abigail shrugged, shifted the baby to the other breast, and continued her conversation with him.

"Auntie Hannah is such a sleepy-head. We'll let her sleep for a just a little while, won't we?"

Abigail sang soft lullabies to her son and her friend until the sun had risen enough to penetrate through the cracks in the walls of the house. She laid the baby down on her mat and gingerly rose to her feet.

"It will feel good to be out in civilization again!" She stretched every muscle from head to foot and left the room to take care of the necessities. Her bleeding had almost stopped and she was feeling so much stronger than she had a few days ago. Saul had sent word that they would be leaving for Jerusalem after the Sabbath tomorrow. One more day of rest and then days and days of walking. Abigail could hardly wait to see her family again and talk to Joanna about all that had happened to her over the past year. She took a quick walk to the well, following some other women, and returned with a jar of fresh water to wash with. Hannah was awake and bustling around the room.

"Where is the new gown you made for the baby? We should really get him dressed. The men will be here any moment now."

"Here it is, Hannah." Abigail reached into a bundle she had already packed for their trip. It was not quite traditional, but it had given her something to do as she lay on her bed the past few days. There was enough fabric to swaddle him from head to foot. Just as the women finished wrapping him there was a knock at the door.

Saul stood in the doorway. Abigail's heart leaped and she wanted to run to him and fling herself at him, but Saul strode past her and took the baby out of Hannah's arms.

"My son." He lifted him high for the other men to see. "He will be named Aaron, after his great-grandfather." The rest of the men came inside and patted Saul on the back, offering their congratulations, then moved aside as the moyel motioned for Saul to lay the baby on the table.

Hannah pulled Abigail back into a corner as the moyel lifted the knife of circumcision and caught her as she fainted at the baby's cry of pain.

Chapter 10

Tomorrow was the Sabbath. The two women spent hours working in the courtyard, preparing double the food needed in order to carry them through the extra day. They were forbidden to do any work on the Sabbath and even though Abigail was not allowed to go to the synagogue until her days of purification were over, she would still have to sit quietly at home with the baby, not permitted to do anything but take care of the basic necessities.

Abigail sat across from Hannah, a grinding mill between them. They held onto the wooden handle and turned it together in perfect rhythm, watching the flour being squeezed out from between the stones, stopping only to add more barley. Hannah pounded the grain a little harder than necessary before pouring it into the mill as if to chase away her next words.

"Luke says we are going no farther with you. We will spend a day or so here in Joppa getting together supplies, then we must head back to Antioch. He received word that his mother is ill and so we must go back and take care of her."

"Saul told me. He was concerned that I was not yet physically ready for such a long trip back to Jerusalem without you along to take care of me."

"You're young and strong, Abigail. I'm sure you will be fine."

"Hannah, I know you have been worried about little Aaron. But I have seen the bright ones around him and know that he will be fine too."

"Bright ones?" Hannah questioned. She reached out and placed her wrist on Abigail's forehead. "Are you feeling well today?" she teased.

"No, really! I haven't told anyone but you, Hannah. They came to me when I was in such pain during Aaron's birth. Then I saw them again surrounding Aaron during the nights when you were up with him."

Hannah's smile slowly faded. "What did they look like?"

"I can't really describe it. Just like soft bright lights, mostly. Like stars! But they had faces that smiled at me and hands that were cool and gentle to the touch."

"Probably just hallucinations, Abigail. You were pretty ill, you know."

Abigail shrugged. "I don't know what they were, only that they made me feel…well…safe, I guess."

Hannah placed her hand on Abigail's as if to bring her attention back to reality. "In any case, do you remember what I showed you about taking care of Aaron if he stops breathing? Or if he trembles?"

"Yes, Hannah, I remember." Abigail gave Hannah an affectionate hug. "But I know my God won't let him die. Saul needs a son to fulfill his mission in life and God gave him Aaron."

Hannah just shook her head. "I hope so, for the sake of both of you…"

"You never told me about your children, Hannah. Do you have any?"

Hannah laughed. "Oh, yes, quite a few. Ten, although the youngest one died in her second year. Luke used to joke about keeping track of them all. Sometimes he would come home with a few that weren't ours, they had just been gathered up with the rest of the boys! What fun we had!"

"Where are they now?"

"Oh, they're all grown up and married now, most of the boys are soldiers in the Roman army and stationed in Antioch. Only the eldest is studying to become a physician like his father."

"And the girls?" Abigail prodded.

"Only two of them and they are both married to successful merchants in Antioch."

Abigail sighed. "What a wonderful life you have had, Hannah."

Hannah didn't answer right away. Her hands stopped pounding and she grew very pensive. "Now I have something to confide in you, Abigail. It may sound as strange to you as the story of your bright ones did to me."

Abigail leaned forward slightly in order to hear the words.

"All through the years I have felt like there was something not quite right, that something was missing from my life. I still feel that way. I should be grateful to the God of Jacob that he has blessed me with so many children and a life of ease, but it seems like I'm waiting for something that eludes me and I don't even know what it is!"

It was Abigail's turn to take Hannah's hand in hers. "It doesn't sound strange to me, Hannah. Sometimes I feel the same way. I used to run off as a child to a place near my house I called my special garden and just sit for hours. I would pretend that I could talk to God just like Moses did by imagining that He was in the bushes." She giggled. "It helped a little. When you come to Jerusalem I will take you there!"

Hannah smiled. "I think you're right in a way. I haven't thought about God in years—since I married a foreigner and stopped going to synagogue. One of my sons was stationed in Jerusalem several years ago and told us a story about a man there who pretended to be God, not just talk to him. He carried the charade a little far, in my opinion."

She shivered and continued. "My son said that the Sanhedrin finally voted to have him crucified and arranged to have the Roman soldiers arrest him for treason. This man never changed his story, even through all the beatings and humiliation they put him through. My son thought these Jews were crazy. They were killing a man who really hadn't done anything. In fact," she whispered confidentially, "he thinks that this was the same man that had been traveling the countryside healing thousands of people. That part interested my son since his father is a healer also. Why our people would want to kill someone that was helping them is beyond my comprehension. Let him pretend to be God if he wants to, as long as he is doing good, right?"

Abigail was staring at Hannah with one hand over her mouth. "I was there! The man's name was…let me see now…Joseph? No. It was a common name. Yeshua. That's it! It was Yeshua."

Hannah nodded. "Yes, that's the same name that my son told me. What do you know about the story?

"Well, not much. I was very young and my parents always sent me off to play when anyone came to the house with shocking news like that. But I do remember hearing from my friend Joanna that a man named Yeshua had been crucified and the whole city being in an uproar over it. We tried to sneak off and see it but her brother caught us and made us go home."

Hannah thought for a moment. "There was more to the story. Luke says that some claim Yeshua was dead for three days and then came back to life—that they actually saw him. Now, as a physician, Luke knows that is absurd, but he is fascinated with the possibility that someone could be beaten, crucified, and stabbed—my son said that one of the soldiers with him shoved a spear into Yeshua's side as he was hanging on the cross—and yet survive. He wanted to go to Jerusalem to talk to this man and examine him to find out how such a medical miracle could have taken place. He also hopes to learn from him more about the healing techniques he used on so many hopelessly ill people. Unfortunately, that will have to wait since we must return to Antioch…"

"Oh, Hannah, I never heard that part of the story. The part about him still being alive, I mean. I'll have to ask my friend Joanna when we arrive in Jerusalem. If anyone will know, she will!"

"Well, I thought that if this man was such a great healer he could tell me what is missing in me to make me feel the way I do. Perhaps I am ill."

Abigail jumped to her feet, spilling the grain that had fallen into her lap. "Do you really think you are sick? And here you have been waiting on me hand and foot! How selfish I've been! Here, you go rest and I'll find your husband for you." She threw her arms around Hannah's matronly body in an apologetic embrace.

Hannah pulled one arm off at a time, motioned for Abigail to sit beside her, and tried to explain. "No, not ill in that way. In here." She pressed a worn hand over her heart. "I'm waiting for something that doesn't come and the waiting makes me sad sometimes, that's all. Please don't worry, Abigail. I was hoping we would find the answers in Jerusalem and now it looks like I'll just have to wait again. It's all right. I'm used to the waiting."

A small squeak in the corner brought both women to their feet. "I'll get him. I've got to get used to doing this on my own." Abigail picked up her son and kissed the nose that was so like his father's. She pushed aside her tunic and snuggled Aaron against her breast.

Hannah gathered up the flour and began mixing it with oil to make bread for their supper. The Jewish community in Joppa had seemed to appear from nowhere for the celebration of the circumcision of the son of the famous rabbi Saul, and there was still plenty of meat left for a nice stew for tonight's dinner. There were bound to be several people stopping by to see Saul for spiritual advice or to see her husband for a salve or some other medicine.

Abigail would usually sing to Aaron as he nursed, but tonight she watched Hannah bustling around, busy with dinner preparations, and she didn't feel like singing. They would have one more day together and then she might never see her again. She wiped a stray tear from her face and made a solemn promise to herself. "If I can find this man Yeshua in Jerusalem to help Hannah, I will do it. I will be brave and ask him if he would write to her husband in Antioch with the cure for her heart-sadness. I'm sure he will know what she is looking for." She brushed away the perspiration moistening Aaron's hair with her free hand. "We will find him, little one. We must."

Chapter 11

She couldn't stand even one more mouthful of dust. Sirocco, the hot wind, was chasing them. There was no escape, no relief. They had walked a long way and even though the baby was heavy on her back, her feet were sore and tired, and the sun beat down mercilessly, it was the dust that made her want to crawl underneath a rock and die. It was evil dust, coming through the pores of the cloth covering her face and choking her, robbing her of the breath for which she was so desperately fighting.

"Saul. I can't go on. Saul? Where are you?" Abigail strained to see the road ahead. For a moment she panicked, then Saul appeared in the middle of hazy, wavy lines over the top of the hill just ahead, coming back toward her.

"Abigail. Look!" There was an excitement in his voice that hadn't been there for a long time. It was the prodding that Abigail needed to keep her feet moving, step by slow step, until she reached the crest of the hill where Saul stood gazing across the valley. There were hundreds of sheep grazing peacefully in the shade of several large trees and a shepherd who paused in his flute playing to wave at them. Abigail let her gaze linger only a moment, then caught her breath at the sight just beyond. It was a steep path leading up a rocky mountainside toward a great city surrounded by walls.

"Jerusalem! Oh, Saul, we made it to Jerusalem!" Now the dust was no longer an evil to her. It was home. She took a long, deep breath of air and followed her husband down into the valley, then up the path toward her family and friends.

They wound their way through the crowded streets. Saul paused at the gates to the temple. Duty to wife and desire to be in the temple tugged him in opposite directions.

"Saul! Is that really you?" A voice from his past broke into his reverie.

"Benjamin! It is good to see you!" The two friends greeted each other warmly. They were dressed almost identically, the long fringes of their mantles nearly touching the ground.

Abigail stood impatiently in the background, bouncing Aaron up and down on her hip, trying to quiet his tears. He was not happy with all the noise and bustle around them and needed to be changed and fed. And there stood her husband, oblivious to their need, chatting away with an old buddy, obviously a Pharisee as well, judging by the size of that phylactery on his forehead. Why did the men do that anyway? It looked awfully uncomfortable. Surely it was better to memorize the Scripture than to carry it around in a box strapped on your head all day. Most men didn't leave it on all day, though. Just in the morning for the reciting of the Shema. But her husband had to do everything more than anyone else, had to be the best, the most devoted.

Finally, the men turned toward her. She didn't like the way Saul's friend was looking at her—his eyebrows raised slightly over narrowed eyes as if he were evaluating her worth. As what? With one hand she pulled one end of her veil down over her forehead and across her face and covered Aaron protectively with the other end.

"She is my wife, Benjamin. And here is my son." Saul lifted the baby away from her and held him toward his friend for approval.

Benjamin clapped his friend on the back. "You have done what you said you would always do, my friend. A wife—and a beautiful one at that." His eyes glanced in her direction appreciatively. "A son, and now an appointment to the Sanhedrin. Well done, Saul. Well done."

"Thank you. And what about you? Where has God's path taken you?"

"I will be joining the Sanhedrin with you. You didn't think I would let you get in ahead of me, did you?" Benjamin joked. "Come with me now. We will go meet the others. They are gathering already for study and debate. Surely your wife knows her way home and my servant can carry your bundles for you."

Saul smiled in relief. God had provided a way again. "Yes. That would be fine. Abigail, I will come for you at your father's house when I am done here." He handed his bundles to the servant and walked with Benjamin toward the temple.

Abigail sighed and led the way. She wouldn't let Saul's desertion dampen the thrill of her homecoming. Soon she would be able to place a grandson in her mother's arms and chat with a friend she hadn't seen in a long time. She and Saul had the same desires, after all. Their friends were different ones, but loved just the same. Saul's behavior was thus excused in her mind and the issue resolved.

She was almost to her parents' door when all of a sudden there was a scream of joy followed by the shattering of a clay pot off to her left. "Abigail! Abigail! Oh, ouch, oh. Abigail! Over here! Ouch. Oh, Abigail!"

Abigail almost dropped her baby in her haste to embrace her friend. "Joanna! It's so good to see you!" She took a step back. "You've broken your water jar and cut your feet."

"Oh, only a little! You're back! Are you here to stay? Where is Saul? Ooooooh! You have a baby!" She gently took Aaron out of Abigail's arms and cooed to him.

Abigail laughed. "Come with me, Joanna. Let me wash your feet and I'll tell you everything!" She sensed another's presence nearby and looked up into a face glowing with a kind of love she hadn't experienced in a long while.

"Mother!" She ran the few steps it took to fling herself into her mother's arms. "I'm home! I'm really home!" Her mother's arms were just long enough to wrap completely around Abigail and hang on as if she would never let go again. When she finally did, she gazed into Abigail's eyes with concern.

"You don't look well, Abigail. You're so pale. Hasn't Saul been treating you well? Oh, I never should have agreed to this!"

"You did the right thing, Mother. Saul's treated me just fine. I've had a baby! It was a hard birth and then a long trip home, that's all. I'll be better after I've had a rest."

Her mother clasped her hands to her heart. "A baby? A son? Or a daughter? Oh, let me see!"

Joanna came forward and handed Aaron to his grandmother. "He's a little soggy." She fanned the front of her tunic, trying unsuccessfully to dry the wet spot the baby had left there.

Grandma didn't care. She cradled the baby close to her and kissed his head over and over again. Aaron's little cries of protest sounded like music to her ears. "I'll change him for you, Abigail. You rest here and talk with Joanna for a while."

The girls sat together on a bench in front of the house. "I'm sorry about the wet spot, Joanna. I should have warned you."

Joanna laughed. "It's all right, Abigail. I have three of my own. I've had wet spots before. They dry."

"Three children? You've only been married two years. How could you have three children already?"

"The first were twins! A boy and a girl—Jesse and Mary. And the last is a girl, Ruthie. She's about the same age as your Aaron. Perhaps we should persuade our husbands to arrange a marriage between them!" They giggled together just as if they had never been apart.

"Tell me about Stephen. Is he a good husband?"

"Oh, he's wonderful! He treats me like an equal! It's just amazing, but I've gotten quite used to it. It annoys some of his friends but no one says anything because they like him too much and are willing to overlook that fault in him, most of the time. I try not to take advantage. Tell me about you. Are you happy with Saul, or do you still see handsome strangers in gardens?" Her tone was teasing but there was real concern in her eyes.

"You remember that?"

Joanna nodded. "Every time I thought of you over these years I hoped that Saul was able to erase the memory of that other man from your mind. I was worried about you."

"Do you remember my wedding?"

"Of course! Like it was yesterday! I'd be surprised if you do, though, since you had your eyes tightly shut through the whole thing."

"I was hoping it was a nightmare that would go away, but when I finally had the courage to open my eyes, I saw the face of the stranger smiling at me."

Joanna looked puzzled. "What on earth are you talking about?"

"The stranger I fell in love with in the garden was Saul."

Joanna's hand covered her open mouth, her eyes wide with delight. "No! Stephen always says that God works in mysterious ways, but this is weird—in a good kind of way, of course. And has he been the angel you thought him to be?" Her voice hinted that she would like to know the marriage secrets they shared.

"Oh, Joanna. I can't tell you that!" She flushed. "But I can tell you he's made me very happy. And you? Are you...happy?"

"Oh, beyond belief! I told you he treated me like an equal..."

"Help! Help!" Hearing her mother's screams, Abigail jumped to her feet and raced into the house.

"The baby! He's dead. He's dead! Oh." She rocked back and forth with the baby, lifeless and gray, in her arms. Abigail tried to grab him away.

"Let me have him, Mother. Let go!" She wrenched him from her mother's arms and gave the bottom of his feet a hard smack.

"Abigail, what are you doing?" Joanna tried to hold on to one of Abigail's arms while her mother tried to snatch the baby back.

"No, you don't understand! Let go!" With strength born out of a mother's love, she shook herself free, picked up the baby and ran outside, jiggling him and calling his name. "Aaron, Aaron, wake up!" She gave his bare feet another smack and held her breath as she watched him take a shaky breath of his own. He shivered and breathed, shivered and breathed, one tiny hand help upward as if reaching for someone just beyond where he lay. Abigail held out a finger and he grasped it. She rocked him back and forth, praying over and over through tears of desperation, "God help him. God be merciful. God help him. Hannah, I need you!" Gradually the gray pallor was replaced by pink and the shivering stopped. He lay still and quiet in her arms, exhausted but alive. It was only then that she noticed the two terrified women standing behind her, clutching each other, not understanding the scene before them. The silence stretched unbroken between them for what seemed like an eternity.

Joanna came and knelt down beside Abigail, putting her arms around her. She wiped away her tears with a corner of her cloak and stroked her hair with tender compassion, not speaking, just understanding the pain.

Abigail reached for her mother, who came hesitantly, apologizing, "Abigail, I'm sorry. I don't know what I did. It's been a long time since I've had a baby around. I must have smothered him, holding him too close."

"No, Mother. It wasn't you. It's not your fault at all. It's mine. I should have told you." Abigail began to sob. "This is not the first time Aaron has had a seizure. God is punishing me again. Today I was grouchy at the end of such a long trip and angry at Saul for keeping me waiting at the gate of the temple while he gossiped with an old friend of his. I should never have gotten angry, especially in front of the temple!"

"Abigail! God isn't like that!" Joanna was horrified.

"I know what I am talking about, Joanna. Saul has taught me about God and his judgment of sin. God cannot look on sin nor does it go unpunished."

Abigail's mother was angry. "Sin! I am a perfect wife all these years, yet I lost many babies. I never complained, always finished my work on time, always went to temple and prayed and offered sacrifices with your father. Where is my sin? Where is God?" She spit on the ground. "I believe God leaves us alone and things just happen, that's all. Or perhaps it is my sin today that has caused this. I was the one with him, after all. No, you should never trust such a horrible old woman with him again."

Abigail looked lovingly at her sleeping baby. "I just know it's not Aaron's fault that these things happen to him. And it's not your fault, Mother. Here, take him inside with you, out of the sun. See, I trust you with him. He's sleeping peacefully now and won't wake for a while." She handed the baby over to her mother. "But, please, Mother, let's not tell anyone else about Aaron's problem. Even Saul is not aware that Aaron gets like this sometimes. I don't want him to ever know. It has to be a secret! People might blame Saul for a child that is not perfect."

Her mother took the child. "Problem? What problem? My grandson is a perfect child." She went into the house as if nothing had happened.

Joanna had been uncharacteristically quiet. Abigail turned to her now. "Surely, you are not blaming yourself for this...are you?"

"No. Just thinking about what you said about sin and the punishment of God. And what your mother said, too, about God leaving us alone. It seems we have two choices. God either is angry with us or ignoring us. Is that what Saul has been teaching you?"

"Well, he doesn't exactly put it like that, but, yes, in a manner of speaking. If we are good, God ignores us and lets us alone. If we sin, God must punish us. I try to be good but sometimes I can't help what I feel. It's like I'm always running away from God so he can't find out how horrible I've been."

Joanna sat pensively for a while, not speaking.

"Abigail, I don't know how to tell you this because I don't want anything to come in the way of our friendship..."

"How could anything come between us? We've been like sisters from birth!"

"Do you remember when we were kids I tried to get you to go see a healer that had come to Jerusalem but my brother stopped us?"

"I remember that! That was the first time I ever heard you lie!"

Joanna wrinkled her nose. "Yes. And last. I may not have shown it, but I was crushed that my big brother was angry with me. I never wanted to disappoint him again. That day we came through the garden on the way home and saw my Aunt Salome running back toward the city. You went home, like the good girl you were, and I went the opposite way, as usual, to see why she was running and what had happened."

"I vaguely recall that. Did you ever find out why?"

"Yes. It was a strange story but I got punished when I got home late that day and for some reason forgot all about it until just recently."

"So what was the story?"

"I followed my aunt to the home of one of her friends. There was a man there who had her little daughter cradled in his arms. I think she was very sick because the women were crying. This man said something I couldn't hear and then gave her back to her mother. I ran home and never told anyone I was there."

"It was the healer! The one we snuck away to see!"

"Yes, I think so. My parents didn't talk about it much but my aunt would sometimes tell me stories of miracles she had seen. Unfortunately this healer did something that our religious leaders didn't like and wanted to have him crucified."

Abigail gasped. "How awful!" She realized with a sinking feeling that this was the one she had promised to seek out for Hannah, and for Aaron. "What happened?"

"Well, my aunt said that she had gone with a couple other women to the tomb of this same man three days after he was crucified with spices to anoint the body. When they got there they saw another man who was wearing a white robe and glowing like light from head to foot. They had been worried about moving the stone out of the way when they got there but were relieved to see that this shining man had already done it for them. Actually, he was sitting on it and appeared to be waiting for them to come. He told the women that Yeshua, the crucified one, was no longer dead, but living, and that they should go tell his disciples. They checked to make sure then ran back into the city to do as he said. That's when we saw them."

"I heard some of this story before. The woman who helped deliver Aaron on the ship told me that she and her husband were coming to

Jerusalem to check it out and talk to this man Yeshua. They weren't able to come all the way so I promised her I would look for him and see if he would write to her husband. Do you know where he is?" Abigail asked hopefully.

"In Heaven."

"I thought you said he wasn't dead."

"Oh, he was, then he wasn't, and now he's gone but he's coming back."

"Joanna, you're not making sense! Did he just have a seizure like Aaron's and not really die? Where did he go and when will he be back?"

"He went to Heaven and I'm not sure when he'll be back."

"How can he not be dead and be in Heaven at the same time? This is nonsense. Your aunt must have made up the whole thing."

Joanna shrugged. "There are a lot of people with the same story. They say they saw him after he was supposed to be dead, walking around, talking with people. And there are quite a few who say they saw him float right up into the clouds and that he told them he was going to Heaven to prepare a place for them and that he would be back."

"A-huh." Abigail rolled her eyes.

"These are respectable people, Abigail, not crazies."

"Well, you've got to admit, it does sound awfully strange! Surely you don't believe all this."

"I'm thinking about it. Stephen says it is true and that it is all possible because Yeshua is the Messiah—actually God's son in human form who came here to save us."

"Save us from what? The Romans? We're still under their authority. It didn't work, so how could he be who he claimed to be?"

"No, not the Romans. He came to save us from the consequences of our sin. You said that Saul told you that God cannot let sin go unpunished. Well, he didn't. You know how our sacrifices at the temple must be pure and unblemished?"

"Yes. Saul says God demands a holy sacrifice."

"That's right. But if you think about it, there is no truly holy and pure animal for sacrifice. It just could never be enough so God sent his son, truly holy and pure since he was God, as the sacrifice."

"That's horrible! Why would he ever do that? I would never let anything happen to Aaron! I can't imagine God letting anything happen to his own son, if that part is even true!"

"He loves us."

"God loves us? Oh, no, I don't think that is right. We are his chosen people and he will use us to set up his kingdom, but I don't think you could say that he actually loves us. He doesn't even know us, as a person, I mean. I'm not sure I would even want him to love us. You say God loved his own son and look what he let happen to him. It doesn't make sense, Joanna."

"Do you love Aaron, Abigail?"

"Oh, yes, with all my heart!"

"I saw what you did to make sure he lived this morning. You didn't let me or your mother interfere with what you knew was best for him even though to us it looked like you were hurting him."

"I would do anything, anything to protect my son."

"Even give up your own life?"

"Yes! I would rather die than see my son die."

"One other question: Who created us?"

"Why God, of course."

"So we are his children?"

"In that way, yes."

"Abigail, I believe that God feels the same way about us that you feel about Aaron and that I feel about Jesse, Mary, and Ruthie. He loves us as his children. Yeshua was not just God's son. He was God himself. God would rather die himself than see his children die. So, he sacrificed himself to save us from a spiritual death."

"You mean, Sheol?" Abigail's voice was hushed.

"While his human body was dead three days his spirit fought with Satan and won! He came back from Sheol and returned to his rightful place in heaven. If we believe in him, he says that when he has prepared a place for us, he will come back and take us with him. Imagine! Living with God."

"I don't know, Joanna. This all sounds very strange to me. Where did you learn all this?"

"Stephen explained it to me. He tells it much clearer than I can. Why don't you and Saul come for dinner and we can talk some more?"

"I'd love to. I'll ask Saul when he comes home."

"I'd better get back to my children. Little Ruthie is probably screaming for her dinner about now and there are some things that grandmas just can't do."

Abigail laughed and shrugged off a nagging feeling that Saul might not be pleased with the developments here as she hugged her friend goodbye. Yeshua was a common name. Surely this loving one wasn't the same one Saul had been raging over. No. Impossible.

Chapter 12

There was something about his smile that instantly put Saul at ease. After his exhilarating day at the temple debating the mysteries of God and trying to make a good impression on his elders, this simple, genuine smile was refreshing. No pretense here, just a man willing to share a meal with a stranger. Saul instinctively knew that here he could relax.

The giggles of the women in the background as they prepared the evening meal, the children and animals running around underfoot, even the rain beating on the roof only added to the charm of this household. Saul couldn't ever remember being in such a nice place. His own childhood home had been secure but he had never felt at ease there. There was always more he should be doing or learning to make his father proud of him. A goal that was always just beyond his reach. Until now, of course. He was Saul of Tarsus, a Pharisee among Pharisees, highly respected rabbi and member of the Sanhedrin to his family and peers. But here in this house he was just Saul, husband and father, a stranger to them, but welcome as he was.

"Welcome, friend Saul." The quiet, gentle voice seemed out of place coming from the tall, lithe man standing in the center of the room, trying to free one leg from the grip of an unsteady toddler. Successful, he grasped Saul's hands in his, smiling broadly.

"Thank you, Stephen. I am grateful for the meal after such a long trip. We haven't yet had time to settle in and purchase household supplies." Saul carefully removed the leather phylacteries, the small boxes that held his precious scripture close to him, from his forehead and left arm and dipped his hands in the cool water Stephen provided. The two of them washed the day's dust from their hands and faces.

"Tell me about your journey. Did you have any difficulties? What is the news from Tarsus?"

With Stephen's encouragement, Saul found himself talking freely, his usual reserve gone. Stephen was a good listener, never once interrupting with his own opinion on a subject or offering an argument to any of Saul's statements. He seemed genuinely interested in Saul as a person, not in winning a debate or showing off his intellectual prowess. The only other person Saul had had such conversations with was Abigail.

Saul smiled as he thought of her and listened to the song-like quality of her voice as she gossiped with Joanna in the adjoining room. It had been many months since he had let himself think of her in such a fond way. It had been necessary to shut her out, to steel himself against the emotions that threatened to soften him, to get in the way of his success. Since the baby, his relationship with her had become one of merely satisfying a physical need. He was so close to achieving everything he had been primed to do his entire life. No emotion. No threat. No failure.

The atmosphere in the house began to thaw the ice that had surrounded his heart and tear down the barriers he had built around his mind. What was the spell this place had cast on him? What was so different and compelling about this man Stephen?

As the women entered and served the meal, Saul let his thoughts explore Abigail's every movement and he felt a desire for her that was not unlike that of their wedding night. She had been so vulnerable, so trusting, that he had taken great care with her, hoping only to make her happy and caring nothing about himself.

Abigail's eyes met his and opened wide in surprise and pleasure at the message she saw there. Her leisurely movements became a bustle of activity as she hurried to help clean up. Joanna stood with her hands on her hips, staring at Abigail.

"What has gotten into you?" She caught the glance between Abigail and Saul and saw Abigail's blush as she hurried back into the other room.

"I think perhaps our guests are tired after such a long day and wish to go home." Stephen grinned at Joanna. "Why don't you get Saul's cloak so they can be on their way."

She nodded, happy to be a conspirator, and went to get it. Abigail had already wrapped up the sleeping Aaron and was holding him close.

"I am so embarrassed, Joanna. Was it that obvious?"

Joanna giggled. "He was watching you all evening like you were some exotic princess or something. You're lucky, Abigail, that he loves you so much."

"Yes, I guess I am. Although, since Aaron was born, I had been wondering if he liked me at all. I thought maybe he was angry at me because the birth was difficult and I took so long to recover."

"He obviously doesn't feel angry now. Go home with him. There's not much left to do here." Joanna gave Abigail a quick hug. "I'm glad you're back. I'll see you at the well tomorrow just like old times!"

Abigail followed Saul out into the damp night as they walked the short distance back to their house. He watched as she put the baby down, still sleeping, then shut the door, pulled her close and removed her wet clothes layer by layer. He stood back for a moment and saw how she stood exposed and unafraid both physically and emotionally, trusting him and loving him completely. He shivered as she came to him, holding nothing back. It made him ashamed of the way he had ignored her these past few months and he made a vow in his passion to protect and cherish the wife God had given him.

Afterward, they held each other and talked late into the night. Saul stroked Abigail's hair as he spoke of the rabbis he had tried to impress that afternoon and the way Benjamin had helped ease the tensions there. He seemed to know everyone. There had been an argument in progress about The Way, a group of fanatics that believed the Messiah had already come. Saul had been more than willing to join in. Funny that Gamaliel had been absent. Saul had hoped to find him there. Perhaps tomorrow.

Abigail, contented, listened sleepily to the happy drone of her husband's voice.

"I liked Stephen. There was something different about him. I've never met anyone quite like that before. Did you know him as a child?"

"Mmmm," Abigail mumbled. "He was always nice. I'm glad Joanna married him."

"Is he a potter, too? Like her father?"

"No. A goldsmith, although I've always thought of him as a scholar like you since Joanna says he talks about God a lot."

Saul was surprised. "He does? We didn't talk about the Scriptures at all tonight."

Abigail smiled and snuggled as close as she could, enjoying the warmth of her husband as he held her. "I noticed that. Actually, I was hoping he would. Joanna told me a strange story today about this man who supposedly was the Messiah but he died, then came back to life again, then left by floating off into the sky saying he'd be back to get us when he'd finished preparing a place for us. She said Stephen could explain it better than she could since she wasn't sure she understood it all. Stephen believes it, though."

Even with only moonlight shining through the cracks, Abigail could see the veins begin to throb on Saul's forehead and feel his muscles twitch in anger.

"The Way," Saul said through clenched teeth.

"What are you talking about?" Abigail lifted her head off his chest, frightened at the change in mood.

Saul, fighting to stay controlled, sat up, pulling Abigail with him. "What did she tell you?"

Abigail told him as much of the conversation as she could remember, hoping that none of this would damage the fragile relationship between them.

"So, Stephen is a member of The Way. No wonder he avoided a Scriptural topic. I knew he was different." Saul slapped his forehead. "How could I have been so blind! It felt like a spell and that's exactly what it was. Abigail!" His voice became urgent. "These people are dangerous. They have taken the Truth passed down to us from generation to generation, the Truth given to Moses by God himself, and twisted and distorted it in a blasphemous way. This man Yeshua was not the Messiah. He's dead. I know that from talking to Benjamin today. He said he was God and our people had him crucified for blasphemy. He got what he deserved. All the other nonsense was made up by these people to deceive us." Saul shook Abigail gently by the shoulders. "Abigail, are you listening? This is important."

"I am listening, Saul," Abigail said quietly, unsure. "But Stephen and Joanna seem to have something inside that we don't have. A peace. A knowledge of something greater than ourselves."

"That's why it is so dangerous, Abigail! Satan is a great deceiver and can disguise himself in many ways—even using a gentle, peaceful spirit to lull us into his trap."

"Trap?"

"Yes. That's exactly what it is. And you must stay away from it, Abigail. I never want to lose you!" He held her close again and ran his fingers through her soft hair, his touch gentle but his words harsh, sending a chill down her back.

"We will not go back into Satan's lair. And you must never, ever speak to Joanna again." He was focused once again. Protective. And he never felt her tears, falling salty and warm, on his chest.

Chapter 13

She hurried to the well early again, although today the sun seemed to be rising a little faster than on other days. Abigail reached up to tuck in a stray hair that tickled her nose and sighed in exasperation. Aaron had awakened at the crack of dawn, eager to practice his new walking skills. He was over two, had already had his weaning party and should have been walking—no, running—and Abigail knew he was anxious to catch up to his peers. Those skinny little legs just didn't have the strength to hold him up. Aaron practiced and practiced, squawking loudly in protest when his frail body didn't cooperate and his feet didn't move as quickly as he thought they should. He had definitely inherited his father's determination! Usually Abigail felt proud of that, but today it had made her late getting started with the day's chores. Now it seemed as if she were racing the sun as she hurried to finish this one last chore. If she didn't hurry she would miss Joanna for sure. It was hard thinking of her as the enemy.

Lost in thought, she filled her pot with the cool water, pausing for a self-indulgent moment to take a quick drink. She smiled as she remembered how spoiled she had become in Tarsus and yet how much more she enjoyed doing the work herself here in Jerusalem. She wouldn't trade her life here for anything! Well, maybe with one small change....

"Abigail," a familiar voice whispered behind her. "I can't stand not being able to come to your house!" Thin arms reached out and gave her a quick hug. "How is Aaron doing?" Joanna pulled her cloak around her head to hide her face and busied herself at the well.

"He's fine. He woke all of the neighbors this morning with his temper."

"I'm so glad we didn't miss each other this morning! Jesse will be four soon and we're planning a celebration in honor of his first haircut. Do you think Saul would let you come? You can't miss it, Abigail, you just can't!" Joanna wailed.

"I don't know...maybe if I wait until he's in a very good mood..."

"Oh, I hope so!" There was so little time to exchange confidences. She babbled on as they filled their jars.

"Guess what! I'm expecting another child!" Joanna looked radiant as she patted her belly. "I felt this one kick this morning. I'm hoping for another boy."

"That's wonderful, Joanna!" Abigail was genuinely happy for her friend, but couldn't help being a little disappointed at her own helplessness to produce another child for Saul. Joanna and Stephen were the ones blaspheming God by their new faith yet they were the ones being blessed by him with more children. She and Saul honored God and had only one sickly child. She felt an anger welling in her heart against this God who would be so unfair.

"Have you thought any more about The Way?" Joanna prodded. "If Saul would just talk to Stephen, I'm sure..."

"No," Abigail interrupted. "I'm not sure I even want him to do that. I'm not sure I want to hear even one more thing about God. I'm sick of this!" She picked up her water jar and stomped back the way she came, not caring about the tears stinging her eyes, not caring if she'd be cursed and die for her attitude, not caring about anything, just wanting her old life back, before this man Yeshua had split it all apart.

She managed to arrive home with all the water still in the jar. Saul was still there, playing with Aaron. Abigail watched for a moment, unwilling to interrupt, as he scooped up their son and tickled his belly. Aaron saw her first and squealed with delight. He pointed to the shelf. "Me eat!" he demanded.

Saul laughed and set him down. "I guess that means it's time for breakfast."

Abigail couldn't stay really angry watching her family. She loved her husband, she loved her son. They had plenty to eat. Maybe life wasn't so bad after all, at least not now. If she just was patient, perhaps Saul would change his mind about her being friends with Joanna.

"I'm taking Aaron with me to the temple today. It's time he learned how to be a rabbi like me." Saul smiled as he said it. "It promises to be a slow day there anyway and, who knows, Aaron may have a few words of wisdom for us."

Abigail raised her eyebrows but said nothing as the two men in her life finished eating and set out for the day's adventures. She brushed aside her nervousness that Aaron would have a seizure and Saul would discover her secret. He'd been just fine for a long time now. There was nothing to worry about.

It was strange not having Aaron underfoot as she swept, but good that he was with Saul. She looked around the quiet and empty house and wished there were other children to take his place.

Saul lifted Aaron onto his shoulders and strode briskly through the busy streets toward the temple. Such a shame to have to push through the crowds and walk past the beggars in order to get to his favorite place. He would love to live sequestered within its walls and never have to leave. Hopefully his son would feel the same way. He already had an inquisitive nature that was easily directed toward study. If not, perhaps there would be other sons....

He paused briefly at the entrance to the temple. It was early and not too many of the men had arrived yet. Saul set Aaron down and held out his finger for Aaron to grasp. They walked together through the doorway.

"Well, well. Starting a bit early with school, aren't we?" Benjamin's voice was cheerful with just a hint of jealousy. His wife had only managed to give him daughters.

Saul patted him on the back. "It's never too early to begin lessons, Benjamin. Why, when I was two, I knew…"

"Enough of this idle chit-chat. We have very important things to discuss today. Very important." An older man swept into the room, obviously upset.

"What is it, Annas?" Benjamin asked.

"They're at it again. Spreading lies not just here in Jerusalem, but all over the country! Soon these lies will spread beyond and ruin us— ruin our traditions, ruin our influence, ruin everything we've worked so hard for here!" The high priest was angry now. "I've sent word to the others to come to Jerusalem. We must have a meeting right away."

"What happened?" Saul sat down on the first stone bench and cradled a sleepy Aaron on his lap.

"Last night two of the leaders of this blasphemous movement were standing in the streets talking to a crowd of people who were curious, and I can't blame them for that, but the things they were saying! Horrible!" Annas covered his ears. "Unbearable!"

"Do they have a new message," Saul asked, "or are they merely repeating their old lies?"

"It's not just what they are saying, that this man Yeshua rose from the dead, but also what they are doing—healing the sick people and beggars. Tricks! Sorcery! Evil!"

Saul glanced down at Aaron and was grateful that he was sleeping peacefully, unaware of the events around him. He spread out his cloak in a corner of the room and laid Aaron down, his attention never wavering from the discussion among his friends. He waved to others as they came in: Caiaphas, John, Alexander, Maaseiah,

Elishama, Peulthai, and many he had not yet met from other cities. There were so many they filled the stone benches nearest the pulpit in the middle of the synagogue.

"I'm glad you could all join us today." Annas' voice was strong and carried well in the packed room. "I'm sure you are all aware of the events in Jerusalem since the last time we all got together a few years ago. I'm afraid the situation has gotten out of hand and needs our immediate attention. Thousands of people are being deceived. Last evening we had two leaders from The Way arrested for spreading their blasphemy. They are now in jail and we must decide what we are to do with them."

Everyone had an opinion. "Send them away."

"No, they will take their stories elsewhere."

"Kill them like we did their great leader."

"Have them beaten—that should scare them off."

"Let's reason with them. Perhaps they will see the truth and turn from their wicked ways."

"They are uneducated men. They will not see the truth."

Annas held up a hand for silence. Gradually the din lessened and the rulers of the Jewish people listened in anticipation to their high priest.

"Let us reason this out in a logical way. First, the message these men are spreading is unacceptable. They are luring people and their sacrifices away from the temple. Thus, we are losing money and soon there will not be enough to support us in the manner which is due us as priests of God."

Heads nodded in agreement. He continued. "Second, they are using trickery to heal those who should be despised by us for their sin, not welcomed with open arms. God has punished them, let God heal them or not. And if he does heal them, they should come to us, like the law of Moses states so clearly, and make their sacrifices. It is we, my brothers, who deserve the credit and respect that these men are stealing from us."

It was silent now in the room as the anger against these common thieves rose steadily.

"Thirdly, God gave us the authority to rule our people. We are their shepherds. It is not the right or responsibility of fishermen to assume that authority. Nor do they have the wisdom to do so. We, who have studied the scriptures from childhood and devoted ourselves to the pursuit of holiness, are the only ones who are able to lead our people."

An angry voice rang out. "Let's crucify them in the same way we crucified their leader!"

A bent figure entered the room silently. A hush filled the room and the men made way for Gamaliel as he hobbled to the front of the room. Even the high priest did not command as much respect as this ancient and wise teacher. "There is no need for blood to be shed."

"How then will we stop this heresy?" Saul spoke up, sure that Gamaliel would have the answer.

"We will hear what they have to say. They should be allowed to defend themselves and their actions and we must be willing to listen. We pride ourselves on reasoning. So, let us reason together." He took Saul's arm and walked to a seat near the back of the room.

The glare of envy and hate in Annas' eyes went unnoticed by most as he spoke with his head lowered. "What do you wish to do, then, my brothers? Do we crucify? Or do we follow the advice of our esteemed teacher, Gamaliel?"

The group of men glanced from one to another, unsure of what the others were thinking. Finally one spoke up in defense of Gamaliel's idea and was echoed quickly by the rest.

"If it is a hearing you want, then we shall have one." Annas waved a hand toward the temple guards. "Go. Get the prisoners."

Most of the members of the Sanhedrin followed the guards outside to watch. Saul knelt beside Gamaliel to wait. "It is good to see you again, Gamaliel. Welcome back to Jerusalem. I have been wanting to talk to you about your last letter to me."

Gamaliel sat quietly, not saying a word.

"It upset me quite a bit," Saul continued, "until I realized that you only wanted to test me, to encourage me to study, to defend the law. That was correct, wasn't it?"

Gamaliel shrugged the shoulders of a weary old man. "Saul, I am more sure every day that I do not have all the answers. It seems the more I study, the more questions I have. The interpretations of the prophets seem so much clearer in light of what these people have to say. It makes sense, Saul. If we lay aside our greed and pride and listen, I believe that we who have always been the teachers will be taught."

Just as Saul opened his mouth to reply, he heard a gurgling sound and a short cry from a far corner. "Aaron!" He jumped up and ran over to where his son had been sleeping. The boy was shaking uncontrollably, saliva oozing from the side of his mouth, his eyes rolled back up into his head. Saul leapt back away in horror. The child suddenly grew still and his usually pale color turned a gray-blue. Saul couldn't move. Not one muscle would respond. He wasn't sure whether to run forward toward his son, or backward, away from the impossible scene. Gamaliel had managed to hobble over and touched Saul's arm.

"Saul."

Saul pointed at the child and then moved unsteadily toward him and picked him up. "My son..." Aaron felt limp in his arms. Limp and heavy. But still breathing. Barely.

Gamaliel gave Saul a gentle push. "Take him out of the temple, Saul. Out into the air."

Saul's muscles kicked into action and he ran with the child out the door and down the street, his feet carrying him to the only place of solace he knew. But it was too late. As he elbowed his way out of the city gates the child in his arms gave one last shudder and stopped breathing. Saul stood in the middle of the garden and looked frantically all around him. He cried out in agony, "My God, my God. Where are you? Why have you deserted me?"

But there was no one there. Nothing. Not even God.

Chapter 14

They had to pry his arms from around the child. In his haze he did not know who they were, only that they came and took his son, his only son, away. There was a burial with many wailing women. Saul put his hands over his ears. When would it stop? Day after day passed, and yet the noise was still there, in his head. Only one woman didn't cry. Instead, she held his hand and walked beside him, as cold and empty as he was.

Abigail! In the eternity that had followed his son's death, he had loved her passionately again and again and, when there were still no more children conceived to take Aaron's place, his heart began to fill its empty spots with bitterness and anger. He prayed fervently at the temple, yet heard no reply. He studied from daybreak to the next dawn yet found no answers there. Benjamin found him asleep in the temple one morning, sprawled out over the scrolls, the candle wax in a pool on the table.

"Saul." He gently shook Saul's shoulder. "Saul. Come on, wake up. I can't stand to see you this way. What question torments you? Let's talk about it together."

Saul wiped the sleep from his eyes and sat up, slouching in despair. "You may be right. I can't seem to think straight." He paused for a moment. "What bothers me is this: What have I done to be cursed by God?"

"What do you mean, cursed? God has blessed you, my friend! He's given you a place of leadership among his people—he has chosen YOU, in the same way he chose Moses and Abraham."

"He has taken my son."

Benjamin sat down beside his friend and put a comforting arm around his stooped shoulders. "Sometimes leaders suffer for the sins of their people. It may be that God is angry at The Way and perhaps even at us for not stopping them from spreading this heresy."

Saul sat silently and Benjamin waited. He knew that Saul's thoughts were already leaning in the same direction and now he gave him time to let the idea twist through his mind and anchor its poisonous tentacles firmly in his heart. He watched in delight as the light slowly dawned in Saul's eyes.

"You're absolutely right!" Saul slammed his fist on the table. His deep voice echoed through the empty room. "And I know just what to do about it." He stood up, straight and tall again, and walked resolutely from the room. He did not see Benjamin smiling to himself and could not hear him whisper gleefully that with Saul's leadership they would soon be rid of the menace and back in control again.

Saul went all the way to Gamaliel's door without stopping. His new mission gave him a strength and endurance he hadn't felt in a long while.

"Gamaliel!" Saul pounded on the door. "Gamaliel!"

The door opened slowly and the old, old man came into the courtyard.

"Saul, what is so urgent? Has something happened to Abigail?"

"No, no, nothing like that. God has given me a special mission and I wanted to tell you since you were the one who got me studying about this whole thing in the first place."

Gamaliel leaned against the wall, listening.

"It's about The Way. I am to wipe out its existence by educating the people. I will begin this Sabbath teaching against its heresies."

"Saul," Gamaliel began. "While you were in mourning many strange things have been happening here." He settled himself on a bench and leaned forward in earnest. Saul sat at his feet, the pupil again.

"A few days ago several of Yeshua's apostles were arrested. For what? They healed a few people, talked about loving others. Nothing we would consider a crime, except they defied our orders not to preach that this man Yeshua was, no *is*, the Messiah we've been waiting for."

"There is their sin, Gamaliel! The Messiah has not yet come. Nor was Yeshua God, as they claim. Let them stay in jail until they admit that."

Gamaliel nodded. "Perhaps they are wrong, Saul, but there is the possibility they are telling the Truth. One must look at both sides of an issue in order to fully understand it. These men were in jail for a very short time, let out by an angel of the Lord, so they say." He held up a hand to stop Saul's protest. "The facts: They were put in jail by the temple guards who stayed outside all night to make sure they did not escape. At daybreak the same men were in the temple courts preaching again. How did they get out? And without anyone seeing them leave? I was there, Saul, with the others of the Sanhedrin in the morning. The jail was locked up tight and the guards were still outside. But our 'criminals' were not inside. They were in the temple." He shrugged. "I have no human explanation. So, perhaps they are right after all and God *is* on their side."

Saul studied Gamaliel's face. "Do you believe this, then?"

"I do not know, Saul. I just do not know. All my life I have waited for the Messiah. For hundreds of years our people waited for the Messiah. Could it be that he came and we killed him?"

"But the prophecies are clear! The Messiah will be our king. He will be the counselor, Mighty God, Prince of Peace. Yeshua brought us no peace, only division among ourselves. He was no king. The Messiah will reign on David's throne. The prophet Isaiah was very clear on this. Yeshua is dead, he has no throne. He could not be our Messiah."

"Perhaps his throne is not an earthly one. Isaiah did not say. But he did say that he would come from Jesse. Yeshua was from that family. He did say that the Messiah would not be appealing to us in his physical form and that he would be despised and rejected by us. And he did say he would be a man who had many sorrows and was well acquainted with grief, that he would be pierced for our sin in the same way we pierce the animal sacrifices at the temple. I heard the horrible story of this man Yeshua being led to his death and could not get Isaiah's words out of my head. They torment me even now. 'He was oppressed and afflicted, yet he did not open his mouth; he was led like a lamb to the slaughter, and as a sheep before her shearers is silent, so he did not open his mouth. By oppression and judgment he was taken away. And who can speak of his descendants? For he was cut off from the land of the living; for the transgression of my people he was stricken. He was assigned a grave with the wicked and with the rich in his death, though he had done no violence, nor was any deceit in his mouth. Yet it was the Lord's will to crush him and cause him to suffer, and though the Lord makes his life a guilt offering, he will see his offspring and prolong his days, and the will of the Lord will prosper in his hand. After the suffering of his soul, he will see the light of life and be satisfied; by his knowledge my righteous servant will justify many, and he will bear their iniquities. Therefore I will give him a portion among the great, and he will divide the spoils with the strong, because he poured out his life unto death, and was numbered with the transgressors. For he bore the sin of many, and made intercession for the transgressors.' And there were others. The prophet Micah said that the Messiah would be born in Bethlehem. Yeshua was born there. The prophet Zechariah said he would be sold for thirty pieces of silver. That's exactly the amount the Sanhedrin paid Judas to lead them to Yeshua in order to arrest him. Even our father David, the great king, described the very words our people said as they cried out for his crucifixion. And why didn't the soldiers break his legs like they do to the others? Is it because he was our perfect Passover Lamb, as he claimed to be? The more I read the prophets and compare them to the events of the past few years, the more convinced I become that Yeshua was the promised Messiah. But if he was, Saul, what do we do now that we have killed him? Will God give us another chance? Or are we now among the damned?"

"Gamaliel, could it be that even you have been deceived?" Saul's eyes narrowed. "I have loved and served the God of our fathers my whole life, kept the law in every aspect. I have been faithful to the only true God. I have always believed that my purpose on earth was to serve God and I have never let anything get in the way of accomplishing the work he has given me to do. Surely God would have revealed himself to me. Surely the Messiah would have come to the temple and been a part of us. It makes no sense otherwise. You, too, have been a faithful servant to our Lord. Will he damn you? Or me? No! No more than he would Moses or Abraham." Saul remembered the words of his friend Benjamin. "We have been put on earth at this time to act again as God's prophets, to warn his people against this evil plot of Satan."

Gamaliel waved a feeble hand toward Saul. "You, go be a prophet. I am too old. May God give you wisdom." His breathing was labored and heavy. "I have talked too much for a man of my age. I must rest now."

Saul felt a little guilty. "Here, let me help you inside." He offered his arm as a crutch but Gamaliel brushed it away.

"Go home to your wife. You look like you could use some rest too. I will sit out here in the sunshine for a while and think."

Saul went on his way, his steps not quite so eager but still resolute. If this heresy was actually persuading his beloved teacher then he must do something about it right away. A plan began slowly to form in his mind. But first he would go home. He was tired. A few hours of sleep then back to the temple to talk to the others.

Abigail watched him go from behind the corner of the house. She had been on her way back from Joanna's and was afraid of being caught. She hid until he was out of sight then silently crept into the courtyard and sat at Gamaliel's feet.

Gamaliel smiled. Here was the daughter he'd never had. She had been coming fairly often to see him, to check up on him really. And he had been able to offer her comfort in a small way just by being there to listen as she wept for her son. With others she was composed, calm, and detached from her pain. But with him she could cry. Today, though, there were no tears. She gazed up at him with a puzzled look.

"I heard what you were saying to Saul. About the Messiah, I mean. Joanna has also been talking to me about him and I've heard what is happening all over the city with his followers. Do you believe what they are saying about Yeshua being the Messiah?"

"Why do you worry your pretty head over such things?" Gamaliel gave her head a little pat. "Do I believe? Ah, such a good question. Why do you wish to know?"

"Well, there is something in what they say—and what I heard you say today—that pulls at me. And sometimes, when I look at Stephen as he is talking about Yeshua, his face looks so radiant, so filled with peace. Do you think that was the kind of peace that the Messiah was to bring? Instead of politically, I mean."

Gamaliel laughed. It felt good to laugh. "You are the perfect wife for Saul. Do you also ask him these questions? In secret, I hope."

Abigail pulled at his sleeve. "I need to know, Gamaliel. And I trust you. Do you believe all this? Is it real?"

Gamaliel suddenly lurched forward, clutching at his chest.

"What is it? What's wrong? Help!" Abigail panicked when he couldn't answer. His frail body was not heavy in her embrace. She lowered him gently to the ground and held his head in her arms as he gasped for air. His eyes flickered open, then shut. A smile formed on his blue lips. A peaceful smile. He reached for Abigail's hand.

"Abigail." She leaned closer to hear him. "Abigail...I...do...believe. I...see...him. I see...Yesh...u...a." His voice grew still. His breathing stopped. His grip on her hand relaxed. And he, too, was gone.

Chapter 15

There were many people at the funeral for the great rabbi Gamaliel. Hiring the wailing women was really unnecessary since there were many who were doing a much better job of mourning, weeping with their hearts. He was laid to rest in a small cave outside the city.

Abigail was strangely unmoved by all the weeping and wailing around her. She would miss him terribly, but somehow this death wasn't as painful for her as her son's had been.

Saul wasn't around when Joanna found her way to Abigail's side.

"Are you all right, Abigail?" Joanna's voice was gentle. "You've suffered more from this than anyone, I think. He was like a father to you." She tried to be understanding.

"Joanna, it's the strangest thing. I'm sad, but not devastated by his death. I have an empty place in my life because he's not there, but…" She looked around furtively. "I was with him when he died and he seemed happy to go."

Joanna looked puzzled. "What do you mean? Happy to die?"

Abigail nodded. "Yes. His last words were 'I believe. I see Yeshua.' There was no one else with us. Do you think he saw an angel coming for him or something?"

Joanna smiled. "No. He saw Yeshua. The one I've been telling you about! Our Messiah!"

"Sshh! Not so loud! Someone will hear you!"

"And what if they do? I am not ashamed of my beliefs."

"How could that be possible, anyway? You told me that the Sanhedrin had this Yeshua killed." Her voice was barely a whisper. "If Yeshua can give peace in death, I want to meet him. I want to ask him about Aaron. Do you think Aaron is with Gamaliel now? Oh, I hope so!"

"Abigail!" Saul had seen her and was on his way over.

Joanna turned quickly away and headed off in the opposite direction. "Meet me in the garden. We can talk there!" Abigail heard her and gave a curt nod as Saul motioned for her to follow him. He hadn't seen Joanna. Or perhaps he was just too upset over Gamaliel's death to care. She walked complacently behind him, wondering how long it would be before she could make her escape. She had to find answers to her questions and somehow she knew that Saul didn't have them.

She watched in surprise as Saul strode into the house and came out tugging several large pieces of goatskin he had been saving. He sat down in front of the house without a word and began sewing the pieces together. Abigail was shocked. He was tent making again. What did this mean? Was he giving up his grandiose plans to become...

"Abigail, hand me that needle." Saul's command interrupted her thoughts. She ran quickly to obey. It was always better to keep quiet and stay out of the way when Saul was in one of these moods.

"I must go take these spices to..."

"Go." Saul's reply was terse. He held the sewing laces between his teeth as he struggled to smooth out the skins. His hands were busy, flying here and there, yet accomplishing very little except to keep his mind occupied and work off the anger that had built up inside again. Another death. Yes, Gamaliel was old. But still...he had wanted to discuss the past several month's events and controversies with Gamaliel but had never gotten the chance. He had been too busy debating with Benjamin and the others in the temple. Too busy. Too late.

Abigail hesitated. She felt the war raging within her husband and was torn between a desire to stay and comfort him and the need to know more about this Yeshua person.

"Go!" This time his word was more emphatic and Abigail grabbed a handful of the spices she had prepared and ran. She didn't stop until she reached Gamaliel's burial cave. There were many women there, all with spices to anoint the body. She looked around, disoriented, and then handed her spices to a woman standing nearby and fled. This was not the place she needed to be. She needed to talk to Joanna. She found "her" olive tree in a remote corner of the garden and sank to the ground between two of its great roots.

"Please, please, Joanna, come!" The words were hardly formed in her mind when Joanna approached, cautiously stepping over the gnarled roots of the tree. She sat down beside her friend and handed her a warm slice of bread.

"I thought you probably hadn't eaten all day."

Abigail smiled. "You're right. I haven't. Umm, this is good. Thank you."

"Tell me more about what Gamaliel said," Joanna probed.

"He said he believed in Yeshua. Then he just smiled and was gone."

It was Joanna's turn to smile. "So, Gamaliel did believe after all. We wondered if he did."

"Who's 'we'?"

"All of us that are a part of The Way. There's been a lot of hatred toward us recently and we were wondering where it was coming from, who was stirring up all the anger." She looked sheepish. "We went through the list of everyone we knew that was not a part of The Way to see if maybe they could be the one doing it. Gamaliel was considered a borderline supporter. We weren't sure which way he would go."

"I don't think he knew until the very end." Abigail was pensive. "Joanna, I want to know more about Yeshua."

Joanna spread out her cloak and arranged herself in a more comfortable position. "I don't have time to tell you everything! You should come to our meetings on the first day of the week and ask all your questions."

"Me? They let women speak in the meetings?"

"Yes." Joanna laughed. "You see what I like most about this! Well, not most, but it is refreshing to be listened to and answered honestly."

"What have you learned about Yeshua? Do you believe he was the Messiah? Saul doesn't think so and he gets very angry at those who do." Her hand flew to her mouth. "Oh, Joanna! Do you think Saul is the one who has been making things hard for The Way?"

"His name did come up. But don't worry about it, Abigail. There are many that are a part of us now who were hesitant at first. Gamaliel, for example! And Nicodemus! Both of them are, were, certainly intellectual equals with Saul. He'll come around, I'm sure!"

"How could Yeshua be the Messiah if he's dead? He can hardly rescue us now, can he?"

"But he's not dead anymore, Abigail. Several weeks after he was crucified, he just appeared to a group of his followers, completely whole and very much alive. He went up into heaven through the clouds. I didn't see it, of course, but those who did see told it to us."

Abigail held her head in her hands and rocked back and forth. "This is all very confusing! Maybe Saul is right. I can't understand so I shouldn't ask."

Joanna took one of her hands. "No. You should ask. I'm just not explaining it well at all." She thought for a moment. "Let me try again. Think about the Passover. Each year, in remembrance of God's deliverance of our people from Egypt, we take a lamb like they did, sacrifice it, and catch the blood in a basin. Then we sprinkle the blood on our door posts and the lintel of our house. Because of the blood, the death angel passed by the doors of our ancestors. The blood rescued them."

Abigail listened intently. "Yes. I know all of that."

"Good. It is all a symbol of our ultimate redemption. The lamb is Yeshua. When he was nailed onto the cross and killed, his blood was sacrificed. By our faith in him, death has no more hold over us. We are rescued forever from Sheol. By putting his blood on the lintels of our hearts, so to speak, when the death angel of eternity comes, he will pass over us, and we will not perish like the Egyptians, but we will have eternal life."

"But the lamb had to be perfect. It is impossible for a man to be perfect."

Joanna thought for a moment. "Yeshua was more than a man. He was God yet he willingly took on the form and nature of man, yet remained without blemish or sin. That's why he is no longer dead. How could God die? He would not be God, then."

Abigail sat thoughtfully. "So, then, his human body died, but his God-soul didn't."

"That's how I understand it to be. Except that after he was resurrected from the dead he had a body, a new body, but the people recognized him so it had to be the same body in some ways."

"Saul says he was not the Messiah, that he was an impostor."

Joanna watched the tormented expression on Abigail's face. "And what did Gamaliel say?"

Abigail looked up in surprise. "Gamaliel believed. He was trying to tell me that it was true." Her voice was tinged with excitement. "The death angel passed over him! I was there! Yeshua rescued him! Oh, Joanna, I believe it too!" she realized in amazement. "I must talk to Saul. May I bring him to one of your meetings? Surely if Stephen talks to him he will realize the truth."

Joanna smiled. "Of course. We welcome everyone. This week's meeting is at our house. Come early and you can help me fix some lunch for the crowd."

Abigail stood and brushed the dirt from her robe. "I can't promise, but I'll try. I'd better go. Saul will be getting hungry. Wait till he hears the good news!"

The women parted company and Abigail hurried home. Saul was still there, the tent almost finished. The physical exertion had been great therapy for his frayed emotions and he had calmed down. The look of determination characterizing his face had returned and Abigail knew the storm had passed, a decision had been made.

"You are feeling better?" she asked, pausing to wipe his sweaty brow. Somehow she managed to make every touch a caress.

Saul sighed. "Yes, a little. I wish I had spent more time with Gamaliel since coming here. I feel like I neglected him in some ways. I must honor his memory, though, by doing what I know would please him."

"And what would that be?" Abigail busied herself with dinner preparations.

"I must stop the heresy that threatens the foundation of our faith. The Way."

Abigail gasped. "The Way? Heretical? No! I'm sure you must be wrong about them. Joanna…"

"Joanna again? I thought I told you to stay away from her! I'm not surprised she's a part of The Way. She seems the scatterbrained, rebellious type to me."

Abigail knew she had to step carefully around this one. "Saul, I was with Gamaliel when he died."

Saul paused slightly in his work. "Why didn't you tell me?"

"I was afraid you would be angry at me for being there, talking with him."

"Why would I be angry, unless…what were you talking with him about?"

"We talked a lot about the coming of the Messiah. He rambled quite a bit and I think he sometimes forgot he was talking to me and thought I was a student or something." She swallowed. So far Saul didn't seem mad at her so she continued. "He told me of a prophecy, of Daniel, I think, that predicted the Messiah would come 490 years after the decree to return to Jerusalem. That was five years ago—the exact time this Yeshua appeared here and began doing miracles."

Saul spit on the ground. "Gamaliel couldn't have believed that nonsense. Yeshua was not a king at all. He was a carpenter from Nazareth. That's all."

"Yeshua was from the lineage of King David, born in Bethlehem. And Gamaliel did believe! His last words to me were that he believed and that he saw Yeshua waiting for him."

"Enough! It's bad enough that they defiled an old man in his last days, but they won't get my wife too! I forbid you to listen to any more of this talk. It is my God-given duty to stop the spread of this blasphemy." He folded up the tent he had finished.

Abigail stood frozen in one spot, terror on her face.

"Don't worry, Abigail," Saul continued. "I am not angry at you. What could you know about things like this? You are only a woman. But I have devoted my life to God and am convinced that he has put me here to stop this, and perhaps prepare the way for the real Messiah to come."

"What are you going to do?"

"I will stop these people no matter what it takes. Tomorrow I will go to the Sanhedrin and volunteer my services." There was a deadly calm about him. "Warnings, punishment, prison, and even death, if necessary. The Way must be stopped."

His words echoed in her head as she thought of Joanna, of Stephen, of others whose only crime was believing in Yeshua, like...herself. Saul reached for her with renewed passion. For the first time her body responded to his touch but her mind was far, far away. Somehow, she had to warn her friends!

Chapter 16

"Abigail! Abigail! Come quickly!" Joanna choked back a sob.

"What is it? What's wrong?" Abigail's heart leapt to her throat. The panic in her friend's voice was unmistakable.

"It's Stephen! They've got Stephen!"

"Who has him? Where is he?"

Joanna could barely talk through her tears. "Stephen was on his way to take food to a widow from our group..."

"The Way? You mean she was part of that group?"

Joanna nodded and the tears flowed down her cheeks. "He never got there. They took him away. Oh, Abigail, you have to help me!"

"Who's 'they'?"

"I don't know! These men stopped us and were arguing with Stephen. He sent me ahead with the food and stayed behind. I heard shouting and name calling so I ran away as fast as I could. I was afraid, Abigail! Oh, I should have stayed there! Now I don't know what is happening!"

"Do you know where they took him?"

"I think they took him to wherever the Sanhedrin is meeting. There were a lot of people out in the streets and they told me they heard the men say that's where they were taking him. Isn't Saul there? You have to help me, Abigail! Please!"

"It will be all right, Joanna. Please don't worry. I'm sure they won't hurt him!"

"Oh, Abigail. You don't know how much these people hate us! It's been building up to this for quite a while and I'm terrified for Stephen! Come on, come with me. We have to stop them!"

Joanna tugged at Abigail's sleeve. The desperation on her face was mixed with fear, not for herself, but for the man she loved, the father of her children. What would she do without him?

The two women hurried toward the temple. There was already a large crowd gathered there and they had to push their way through the throngs of people. The shouting pounded through Abigail's head. Why were these people so upset? Abigail felt confused. Stephen was hardly a criminal! He had done nice things for many of them standing here! There was Malachi shouting the loudest. Why, Stephen had helped him last week mend his rotting doorway. And over there was Kareah. Wasn't he the father of the little boy Stephen had cured of some dreadful disease?

"Abigail, I can't hear what they are saying! We've got to go closer!"

Joanna pulled her friend toward the front of the crowd. They were almost there! Abigail looked up.

"There he is, Joanna, look!" She pointed to the steps just ahead of them.

Joanna gasped. "Stephen!"

He was being pushed up the stairs toward the temple, but paused for a moment and looked in their direction. His hands were tied behind his back and a rivulet of blood trickled down the side of his forehead. Joanna reached up as if to brush the hair from his eyes. Stephen saw them in that instant and smiled.

The voices crescendoed behind them. "See how he mocks us with his smile! This man blasphemes our God and speaks out against our law! Punish him!"

Abigail couldn't take her eyes from Stephen's face. It was different somehow. Calm. Serene. Unaffected by the cruelty around him.

Like…like she imagined an angel's face to be. A movement directly behind him caught her attention. It was Saul! She started to wave, to request an audience with him, to explain what had happened, but the look on his face rooted her and she could not move. Her husband's face was filled with anger, hatred, turmoil. She gazed from one face to the other. Tranquility…tumult. Love…hatred. How could two good men be so different?

Saul motioned to two of the most vocal men standing nearby. They shoved Stephen into the courtyard. Saul stood tall and righteous in the bright sunlight, his arms folded across his chest. Joanna threw herself into Abigail's arms and sobbed in anguish. She heard the booming voices of the men, accusing, angry.

"There are men here who say you speak against our laws and even against this temple. Who accuses you?"

"If I may speak, sir." Benjamin slithered silently across the courtyard toward the high priest. He leaned conspiratorially toward the older man as if in conference, yet spoke loud enough for the others to hear. He especially wanted Saul, standing just to the right of the high priest, to hear. "This man is a major organizer of The Way."

A snort escaped from the mouth of the high priest. "Take him! He must be punished for his blasphemy!"

"No wait!" A deep voice echoed through the stagnant afternoon air. Joanna lifted her head from Abigail's shoulder to watch, to hope.

"He must be given a chance to speak first, to answer his accusers."

"You are correct, Nicodemus." The high priest looked surprised to identify the objector. "Speak then, blasphemer, defend yourself." His voice was menacing, sending a shiver through the two women who watched breathlessly.

Stephen stepped forward and spoke to the crowd with a clear and unapologetic voice. His words sounded like gibberish to Abigail as the monologue went on and on, but she could not mistake the security, the knowledge of Truth in his tone. He spoke with conviction and authority about the faithfulness of God even when they, as a people, had been unfaithful. She wanted to run forward, to plead with Saul and the others to let him go, and was just about to break free from Joanna's grip when Stephen turned back to the leaders and spoke harshly.

"You are exactly like the leaders before you! You resist the Truth and the Holy Spirit of God who gives the Truth just like they did. You killed every prophet God sent to us. We were given the Messiah and you murdered him!"

The men listening were furious, clenching their fists, growling like animals.

"Look!" Stephen lifted his shackled hands toward the sky, his face shining. "I see the Throne of God and the Son of Man standing to the right of it. Yeshua!"

Abigail lifted her eyes to see, but was shoved roughly to the ground by the merging crowd, one leg bending awkwardly beneath her. She screamed in alarm and held on tightly to Joanna. The fabric she was clutching so tightly on the sleeve of Joanna's tunic ripped and they were separated as the crowd surged forward, dragging Stephen down the steps and out of the city. The grunts and growls of the men storming by were almost demonic and they terrified her. She crawled from underneath the trampling feet and huddled in a corner of the street, sobbing until she felt a hand tugging at her, urging her to get up.

"Please come with me, Abigail. I have to see what they are going to do!"

"We don't dare go, Joanna. Don't you see how angry they are? They will murder us as well!"

"I have to go! I have to be with him!" Her eyes were wild with determination.

"No. Wait!" Abigail pulled her friend out of the way just in time as more men rushed past them, picking up stones from the street as they went. "It's too dangerous. Think about your children! They need their mother!"

"And I need my husband!"

"We should hide you. They may come after you next. Come." Abigail pulled her down a side street. "I'm sure my father will protect you until this settles down. He's not one to be pulled into such a hateful debate. Let's go."

"Maybe you're right." Joanna relaxed and walked placidly beside her friend. Abigail let go of her arm for a moment to brush the dirt off of her tunic. It was just enough time for Joanna to turn and run swiftly in the opposite direction, toward the gate of the city where they had taken Stephen.

Abigail sighed. This time she would have to follow. This was not a simple scrape Joanna could get out of on her own. She would have to catch up to her and not let her guard down again. She picked up her skirts and limped off after her friend, hoping no one would notice her.

She could see her in the distance. Joanna hadn't gotten far. The crowd by the gate was blocking the way. What were they doing piling up all those stones? She walked a little faster, ignoring the pain in her leg.

"Joanna!" She reached forward and grabbed her by the arm, holding on tightly.

"Oh, Abigail. I just had to be here and now I can't get through!" She sounded hysterical.

"Don't worry, Joanna." Abigail tried to soothe her. "Please, don't worry. Look, there's Saul. If we can just make our way over to him, I'll talk to him for you."

They jostled their way around the mob of people toward where they could see the top of Saul's head. There seemed to be an awful lot of activity over by him as well. They got up close enough to peer through the throng. Abigail's face turned white and she tried to keep Joanna from seeing.

"Abigail, move! We're almost there!"

"No. It won't do any good now."

"What do you mean? We're almost to Saul. Please, hurry!"

"Joanna. We're too late. Let's go back now. I don't want you to see…"

"See what? Oh my God!" Joanna froze in horror. The crowd was breaking up now and moving leisurely back toward the city. Only the two women stood immobilized, staring at the broken and bloody body of someone they could hardly recognize. Abigail looked up at Saul standing nearby. He had not seen her and was calmly distributing the cloaks he had been holding. Cloaks belonging to men who had done this awful thing to Stephen. Joanna saw it at the same time and turned away.

"I'm going to him." Her voice was devoid of emotion. Empty. She knelt near Stephen's lifeless body and began removing the stones that buried his head one by one, laying them in the shape of a cross next to his outstretched arm. As she tugged and pulled at the heavy stones she began to cry softly.

"Joanna, I'm sorry…"

"It's not your fault, Abigail. The Lord's will be done." She finished the pattern of stones, kissed Stephen's bloodstained forehead gently, then stood and slipped off quietly through the crowd. Abigail watched her go, helpless. She turned back toward Saul, not quite believing what had happened. He had finished giving back the garments and raised one eyebrow when he saw her standing there. Benjamin came and took his arm, guiding him back toward the city gates. He went without even a glance back and Abigail stood alone, remembering his words. "Even death…whatever it takes to stop The Way. Even death. Even death. Even death." But why did it have to be Joanna's husband? She didn't feel the tears streaming down her face as she looked once more at the form lying so still beneath the rocks.

Chapter 17

When Saul came home Abigail was there, sweeping the dusty floor. She swept and swept, trying to sweep away the image of the dead man from her mind along with the dirt. She squeezed her eyes shut, trying to forget, but instead saw clearly Stephen's still body with Saul standing over him, calmly passing out cloak after cloak after cloak. She swept harder and faster until she reached the spot where Saul was standing, his arms crossed and a grim look on his face. He reached out to stop her.

"Abigail. I'm sorry you saw what happened today. It couldn't be helped. It was God's will to stop this man from spreading such blasphemy."

Her look was accusatory. "He was Joanna's husband. What will she do now?"

"I'm sure Joanna's friends will take care of her. People like that stick together."

"Who's next, Saul? When does the murdering stop?"

"Not murder, Abigail. Justice. I know you don't understand and I can't really expect you to, but the Holy Scriptures are quite clear on how to treat one who blasphemes the Most High God. We must keep our religion pure! We don't dare disobey."

"But what if what they're saying is true? That God sent the Messiah and we didn't believe. Wouldn't that be as great a sin?" She turned away but Saul pulled her close, his arms wrapped around her from behind.

"Yes, that would indeed be a great sin." Saul smiled. "But we don't have to worry about that since what is being claimed about Yeshua is not true at all." Abigail struggled to break free, angry at her husband, but Saul held her tightly.

"What's this? You have been eating too much lately?" Saul teased, rubbing her belly. His eyes went wide as he felt a little kick against his hand and he let go of her.

Abigail kept her face turned away from him and was silent.

"Abigail, why didn't you tell me? When will we have another son?"

Abigail shrugged and put her hands around her waist protectively. "Still a few months more, I think. I'm not really sure. I wanted to be sure before I said anything..."

Saul let out a whoop and swung her around in a circle. "God is blessing me for being faithful! After all this time another child! I thought it was impossible. Praise God!" He held her face gently in his hands and kissed her.

"Don't worry, Abigail. I will make our world as safe as possible for our family. Those who destroyed Gamaliel and little Aaron by their sin will have no claim on this one. I will make sure of it."

He turned to go and Abigail watched him, tormented to the depths of her soul. Somehow she must stop him. But how? She sank to her knees and began to talk to the God she had just met.

"Yeshua? Can you hear me? I have to whisper so that Saul doesn't hear. So that the neighbors don't hear. I'm so afraid! I believe you are our Messiah just like Stephen said. Please, please make Saul believe too! The killing must stop!"

"Abigail, come quickly! Joanna is having her baby and she's calling for you!" Her mother's voice was urgent. "I think something is wrong."

Abigail jumped to her feet and ran all the way across town, not waiting for her mother who was huffing and puffing behind her. She flew into the house and went straight to the room where Joanna was writhing in agony.

"Joanna. Take it easy. You've done this before! You'll be fine." Abigail smoothed the hair from Joanna's sweaty brow as she struggled with the labor pains wracking her body.

"I'm so glad you're here. Hold my hand! This one is worse than the others." The words came haltingly. Her knuckles were white as she gripped Abigail's fingers. "If I don't make it, this child is to be yours. Take good care of him."

"Joanna! Don't talk like that. Of course you'll make it!"

"I want to be with Stephen."

"No! Your children need you. I need you! Now push!"

Suddenly a lusty cry filled the room and Abigail gently wrapped the baby in the linen clothes they had sewn together just a few months ago. She handed the baby to Joanna and stepped back to let the midwife take over.

"It's a boy, Joanna. A precious boy!" She was thrilled for her friend. "And you made it through just fine."

Joanna smiled weakly. "Thank you for being here, like always. What would I do without you?"

Abigail stroked the baby's face. "Hello, little Joel."

"I've changed my mind, Abigail. He won't be named Joel after all."

Abigail looked puzzled. "But you've had that name chosen for a long time."

"He will be called Stephen, for his brave father. And perhaps he will take over where his father left off." Her look was determined. "I will teach him about The Way."

The whinnying of horses mixed with the familiar sounds outside. Their snorting and pawing was aberrant and ominous. Joanna struggled to her feet.

"You shouldn't get up just yet, my dear." The midwife's tone was worried. "You take it easy. We will see what is happening and come and tell you." She hurried out the door. They heard her arguing with the men outside, pleading for something.

Joanna clutched the baby to her. Her other children were outside and she could hear them crying for her. She leaned on her friend to steady herself and cautiously walked to the doorway. The brightness of the daylight accentuated the paleness of her skin, the hollowness of her eyes. The midwife was gone. There were Roman soldiers and...Saul. She motioned for Abigail to stay inside and gingerly stepped into their view.

"What do you want? Why do you come to the home of a woman who has just given birth?" She held up her infant son. "I am too weak to cause you trouble."

Saul stepped forward. "We are looking for those who defile the name of our God. You are a blemish to our people."

"I have done no such thing. I merely tell the truth." Joanna's eyes flashed with fire. "You didn't believe my husband, why will you believe me? Look into your own heart, Saul, and see the Truth!"

"Enough!" Saul was angry. "Take her to prison and her children with her!"

"No!" Abigail ran out into the street. "Saul, you can't..."

The horses were spooked by this panic-stricken woman, running here and there. They reared uncontrollably.

"Abigail! What are you doing here? Go home right now!"

The dust swirled around them as the soldiers grabbed for the children, snatching one up by his hair, another by her skirt. They were laughing.

"Saul, don't do this!" Abigail shouted over the din.

"I have my orders. We will cleanse the house of Israel! Now get out of the way before you get hurt. Go home!"

"I can't, Saul!" Abigail sobbed. "I'm one of them. I believe!"

"No!" The rage in his voice echoed off the houses around them. He intended to grab her and take her home himself. She was not in her right mind, due to the pregnancy of course. He reigned in his horse sharply, struggling to turn him around, to get near her. More soldiers were coming. There must be about twenty now. They were in the way. Hooves were flying everywhere, making enormous dust clouds around them.

"Abigail! Where are you?" Saul's voice held a hint of panic. He heard screams and nudged his horse in that direction, shouting orders at the soldiers.

"Move out, down the street. This whole section is filled with followers of The Way. Get them all!"

Joanna stood her ground, refusing to give up the infant in her arms. A soldier leaned over his horse and beat her with his whip. She stood unmoving, staring at the tempest raging around her. He beat her again and she sank to her knees, still clutching her baby, trying to protect him from the violence around them.

Abigail screamed again. "Joanna, I'm coming." She weaved in and out of the pounding hooves, choking in the dust. She reached out, almost there, but a soldier snatched her friend up as if she were a rag doll and threw her on the back of his horse. He wrenched the baby from her grasp and threw him to another soldier, who tossed him to another soldier and another down the line. They laughed and mocked, delighted at the fright and chaos they were causing. Finally, the last soldier threw the baby in the dirt and they galloped off after another victim.

Abigail stood crying in the middle of the street. The dust was beginning to clear and she saw Saul searching for her.

"Abigail? Abigail!" He saw her and urged his horse in her direction. A soldier saw her at the same time and raced to where she stood.

"I've got her!" He was young. Inexperienced. Enthusiastic. He lost control, pulled the reigns a little too hard. The huge horse reared, its hooves pawing the air, and came down. On top of Abigail.

Saul watched in horror as time seemed to stand still. He saw the impact as the hooves drove through her skull. He saw her crumple to the ground, instantly lifeless. He saw her blood staining the ground, mixing with the blood of those who had deceived her. And he saw the tiny movement from her belly one last time before she shuddered and was still.

He turned his horse away and galloped crazily up and down the street, ordering mass arrests. Women, children, it didn't matter. They had done this and they would pay.

Chapter 18

He didn't know what they'd done with the bodies and he didn't care. Saul spent his days gathering up blasphemers and every evening on his knees in the temple praying, begging God to forgive his people for their great sin. Night after night he wept with grief over what was happening to Israel and renewed his vow to the God he loved to purge his nation from this insanity. Locked away in a secret part of his heart was a grief too big to ever mention. Abigail. He dreamed of her every night—felt her breath on his skin, her fingers caressing his hair—as if she was still there. If she really had forsaken God and become a follower of The Way, she deserved her death, but Saul was desperately in need of her, his best friend, his confidant, his wife. Saul shook off the memories of her and began to pray. He lifted his hands and began the familiar chants. There was no comfort in the words. He missed…he missed….

Saul shook his head to clear it. He missed something? That was ludicrous. He had God in a way that others could never hope to experience. He was Saul of Tarsus, Roman citizen, a respected Jewish leader, man of God, member of the Sanhedrin, Scriptural scholar—and always right.

Most evenings he was alone but tonight he could feel another presence in the shadows. He peered into the darkness.

"Who's there?"

"It is I, Nicodemus. I did not wish to disturb you. Please, continue your supplications. I will pray somewhere else."

Saul smiled. He liked this elderly Pharisee. He was rather timid for one of his years, but always kind and very knowledgeable in the Scriptures. Some men fell asleep on the rare occasions when Nicodemus spoke in the temple, but Saul enjoyed his gentle discourses on the Scriptures. There was always a thought-provoking question somewhere in the lesson, usually couched in an apology.

"Come pray beside me," Saul said. "I would enjoy the company. What brings you here at this hour?"

"I...I don't know, exactly. I just felt like I should come."

"Perhaps you are as troubled as I am with what is happening to our people."

"You do look like a man with a heavy burden on his shoulders. Perhaps I could help you carry it."

Saul grimaced. "Indeed I am! But I don't think you have the stomach to do what God has called me to do."

"And what is that?"

"Have you been in hiding these past few weeks?" Saul was incredulous. "I must lead the effort to cleanse Israel from its sin of blasphemy. We must repent! I can't believe it perseveres even yet. We have been all through the city, throwing all the known followers of The Way into prison. There must be more somewhere. They are like leaven, contaminating the pure bread of Israel."

Nicodemus was silent, his face flushed with embarrassment. Saul looked at him with astonishment.

"Not you, too?"

"I...I knew Yeshua, you know. I was here in Jerusalem before he was killed. He seemed like such a nice man. He was always patient with my questioning and seemed to have an explanation for all that I asked about his teachings. He knew much more than any of us."

"Do you believe he was the Messiah?" Saul's scowl was deepening.

"I don't know. I haven't made up my mind yet." Nicodemus shrugged with caution. "There is much evidence to support the argument and very little against it, don't you think?"

"Quite the contrary!" Saul was indignant. "The man is dead, not ruling as the Messiah should."

"Um. Well, yes, I suppose you're right. But he did fulfill all the known prophecies about the Messiah."

"Except for a few that said he would rescue Israel! He couldn't even rescue himself!"

"Yes. That puzzles me as well. Although he did tell me once that he must be crucified in order that we might have eternal life."

"That doesn't make sense."

"It is hard to understand what he meant, I admit. He explained it to me by comparing it to what Moses did in the wilderness years ago."

Saul looked confused. "What has that got to do with the situation now?"

"I'm sorry I'm not making this clear! I'm trying to remember exactly what he said. You remember the story about our people wandering in the desert after their narrow escape from Egypt?"

Saul nodded and Nicodemus continued his story. "I think he was referring to the time when they spoke against God and God sent poisonous snakes that bit many of them and they died."

"I don't see how that relates. Unless the sin of our people now is blasphemy and I am a snake sent to punish them."

"Well, that could be, Saul." Nicodemus nodded thoughtfully. "But the solution to our ancestors' problem was that Moses had to make a bronze snake and put it up on a pole. Everyone who was bitten that looked at the bronze snake lived and was saved from death. Yeshua told me he was to be the bronze snake, so to speak, for our people. He would be lifted up, crucified, I guess he meant, and whoever looked to him would live."

"That's the strangest story I've ever heard!"

"I haven't quite figured it out myself."

"What other words of wisdom did he have for you?" Saul sneered.

"Well, now that you've asked..." Nicodemus caught himself. "Oh, I guess you don't really want to hear."

"No, no, go on. I would love to hear this."

"Well," Nicodemus said sheepishly. "He talked about being born again."

Saul merely raised an eyebrow.

"I asked him about that one, too. He said that everyone was born of the flesh but that was not enough. We must also be born of the spirit. He was talking about heavenly things," Nicodemus finished lamely.

"I see."

"He said we are all spiritually doomed and that God loved us and sent his own Son—Yeshua—to die in our place. Like the Passover lamb!" Nicodemus' voice was tinged with excitement. "I think I'm beginning to understand."

"I hope you will not be pulled into this fabrication, like so many others."

"Ah, so that is what troubles you! Who else has believed?"

Saul frowned. "Gamaliel was a believer, you know."

"No, I had no idea! Gamaliel? Um. Very interesting."

"And my wife."

"Your wife? How did that happen?"

"She was persuaded by a friend of hers. And her family too. Her family was…arrested…this morning." Saul turned his head to hide his grief. He must not break.

"Did none of them seek to persuade you?"

"Yes. It seemed like everyone I loved kept pushing and pushing for me to accept this new teaching. Never! I will remain true to my God! He will not find me lacking in zeal for him."

"I'm sure they tried to convince you because they loved you and were just as sure of their position as you are of yours."

"Yes, it's tragic, isn't it? That's why it is so important for me to stop this lunacy before it spreads further. I must!" He pounded his fist into his hand for emphasis.

"Well. I wonder if there might be a spiritual world right along side of this one that we don't quite understand yet. If perhaps our soul is more important than our physical body to God. If maybe it was our soul that Messiah came to rescue. I'm terribly sorry to have disturbed you. Goodnight." Nicodemus slipped out as quietly as he had slipped in. Saul shook off the nagging doubt and felt another brick placed in the load of worry he was carrying. He tried to forget Nicodemus' final words. What had he meant by that anyway? It was late. His thoughts were no longer orderly, but instead swirled around his head in confusion. So, he buried his head in his arms and slept on the temple floor.

Chapter 19

"Saul. Saul, wake up." Benjamin shook his shoulder. "You've done it again! Slept all night in the temple. There must be a law against that somewhere," he joked.

Saul ran his hands through his hair and smoothed down his beard. "Thanks for waking me, Benjamin. There's so much to do today. How many are left?"

"Slow down." Benjamin looked amused. "We've got the ringleaders and most of their followers. There can't be more than a handful left free. The prisons are so crowded I'm not sure we could fit even one more in. Of course, soon some will die and then..."

"We must get them all, Benjamin! We'll use my house as a prison if we have to!" Saul jumped to his feet and threw on his cloak. The mornings were cool now.

"Wait!" Benjamin put up a hand to stop Saul from leaving. "I suggest you get cleaned up first. You look awful—no offense meant, dear brother."

He took Saul's arm and led the way to his own home just a few hundred yards away. He motioned for his servant to bring a large bowl of water.

"Sorry we don't have time for you to go down to the river for a full wash, but this will have to do."

Saul scooped up the cold water with his hands and splashed his face. The servant handed him a towel and then bent to wash Saul's feet.

"There. You look more presentable now. How about a bit of breakfast?"

Quickly the servant brought food. He had learned to be expeditious in order to avoid being beaten by his austere master.

Saul ate hungrily. He had forgotten to eat for several days, caught up in the seriousness of his work.

"You are a good friend, Benjamin. Thank you!"

"Think nothing of it, Saul. We are brothers in every way that matters. I know you would do the same for me."

"Of course I would!" Saul's voice was overcome with emotion. "You are the last friend I have on earth! I would do anything for you!"

"Good." He hesitated dramatically. "Very good."

"What is it? Is there something I can do for you?"

"Not for me. For our God."

Saul stood up tall. "Anything."

"It seems that some of the followers of The Way have escaped Jerusalem."

"I will find them! They must die!" Saul was furious.

"No need to find them, Saul. We know where they are."

"Where? Tell me. I will go myself and bring them to justice."

Benjamin smiled. "Ah, I knew we could count on you. They have run to Damascus. Evidently they are converting many there as well. You will have your hands full. I would go with you, but my wife…"

"I understand completely, Benjamin! Of course you must stay here. I will go."

"You will need help."

"There are a few soldiers who have been loyal. Roman Jews, like me. I will take them."

"The Rabbis in Damascus don't know you. Perhaps they will not believe you when you tell them of this threat."

"I will get letters of recommendation from the high priest. They won't dare hide anyone that way. They will have to give them all up and we will bring them back to Jerusalem and throw them in prison with the rest!" Saul's tone was menacing.

"I have prepared some food for your journey so that you may go without delay. God-speed, my friend."

Saul walked resolutely back to the temple for a conference with the high priest and was on his way out of Jerusalem in a matter of hours.

He listened to the excited chatter of the men with him and the steady clip-clop of their horses along the dusty road, concentrating on his righteous purpose. It was a long ride and he tried to erase from his mind the morose images that kept popping in. So much sorrow. So many deceived. So many dying. He felt the breeze through his hair and thought for a moment it was Abigail, reaching out to stroke his head, to comfort him, to tell him he was doing the right thing.

"Sir. Sir!" A voice broke through his reverie.

"What is it?"

"We are almost to Damascus."

"Good."

"The horses are tired and thirsty and so are the men. There is a well nearby. Might we stop for a while, sir?"

"Lead the way."

"Thank you, sir."

The well was not far. Saul slipped gracefully off his horse and enjoyed the cold, fresh water. It was just what he needed to clear his thoughts and focus again on the mission. He looked around at the men joking and laughing with each other and was proud of their dedication and commitment to him and to what they were about to do. They were crucial in his plan.

All of a sudden the sun seemed to explode around him. Saul fell to his knees, his hands covering his eyes.

"What is it? Are the rest of you all right?" Saul shouted at his men.

The soldiers stopped their joking and looked toward their commander. He was on the ground, hands over his face.

"Sir, what is it? A snake bite? There are some poisonous ones around here. Let me help you."

But Saul waved them away. "No. It's the light. Something exploded. It's burning. No. Just light. Don't you see it?" There was panic in his voice, something the men had never heard. They shook their heads and stood waiting, unsure of what to do.

"Saul!" All of them froze at the sound. There was no one else there. Who was speaking?

"Saul, why are you persecuting me?"

"Where are you? Who are you?" Saul asked. He didn't dare look up.

"I am Yeshua." The voice was kind. "I'm the one you are persecuting."

Startled, Saul looked. For a brief moment he saw him standing in the midst of the great light and knew instantly that it was true. All of it. This was Yeshua. Not dead, but not alive in the same way he was. Better! Much better! He squeezed his eyes shut in horror as a flood of shame washed over him. What had he done? Abigail! Oh, Abigail....

"Saul, get up. Go ahead into Damascus and you will be told what to do."

The light disappeared as quickly as it had come. Saul stumbled to his feet. He opened his eyes and saw nothing. He clawed at his face and his men rushed over.

"Sir, what are you doing? What was that? Who was speaking to you?"

"You heard it, then? It was Yeshua."

The men looked at him in disbelief. Had he gone mad?

"I cannot see. The light blinded me." He groped for an arm in his darkness. "You must take me into Damascus."

Shaken to the core, only understanding that something important had happened, two of the men took his arms and the others led the horses.

"Wait!" Saul stopped short. "First, find the letters!" He rummaged in the saddle bags until he felt the bundle of letters from the high priest. "Here. Burn them. Now!"

Chapter 20

The men had taken him to the house of Judas on Straight Street. The irony of this did not escape Saul. Hadn't Judas been the name of the traitor who had delivered Yeshua to the Sanhedrin? And Straight Street? All this time Saul had thought he was on the straight path—the true path—and yet he had been persecuting those who were actually on that path.

For three days Saul struggled with the demons raging inside of him. He knew the light was real—it had blinded him. But the voice…it must be real because the others had heard it too, but the doubts kept returning over and over, haunting him throughout the days and nights. He could not work, he could not write, he could not speak. He wanted to see no one. He spent the days praying and the nights tossing and turning in his bed. The guilt was overwhelming. Certainly he felt that the blindness was the least of what he deserved. This night was no different. He could not sleep but had no idea what time it was. He only knew it was evening because the servants had bid him a good night a short time ago. His only desire had been to serve his God with all of his heart and being. In his zeal, his conviction that he was right, he had authorized the killing of so many innocent people. How could a just God let him live now? "Oh, Yeshua, I believe in you. But I have wronged you so much. Please provide a way to make this horrible thing I have done right in your eyes," Saul prayed. "But how will you ever accept me? I am not the perfect man I thought I was. I must be a great disappointment to you. I still have this desire to serve you, to obey you," Saul continued. His brooding and pleading gave way to fitful sleep with one more phrase on his lips, "Like Abigail…"

An insistent knocking on the front door woke Saul from a deep sleep. He rubbed his eyes, trying to see through the darkness, forgetting for a moment that he was blind. Reality was still hazy as he struggled to wake from the dream. What a dream! He had met someone named Arnie, no—Ananias, who had touched his eyes and healed him. The knocking continued. Saul shook his head to clear it and called out, "I'm coming." He stumbled to the door and fumbled with the latch. "Who is it?"

A pudgy, normally jovial man tentatively entered the house. Saul extended his hand in welcome. "You will have to tell me who you are as I cannot see you."

Instead of an answer, Saul felt two large, warm hands grab his shoulders. A halting voice spoke, softly at first, as if afraid to be there. "Saul, Yeshua sent me. The same Yeshua you met on the road to Damascus—he sent me to restore your sight and to enable you to be filled with the Holy Spirit."

Saul's blind eyes widened in surprise. "Yeshua is not angry at me? He will not take my life as I have taken the lives of those who have served him faithfully?"

Ananias smiled—and Saul saw it. He waved a hand in front of him. "I can see. My sight is returning." His amazement turned to joy as the fuzzy outline of Ananias' face came into focus. Saul grabbed his face with both hands and kissed his cheeks. "I can see!"

Ananias' smile broadened. "You will have spiritual sight as well. Yeshua himself will teach you through his disciples—the ones you have been seeking. Yeshua told me that you have been chosen by him to carry his name to the Gentiles and their kings, as well as to the people of Israel."

"I will go!" Saul felt real joy for the first time in years. He knew. He just knew that this was the mission he had been seeking. To serve God. To serve Yeshua. To spread the word of the faith that had captured Abigail's heart, the faith Gamaliel had embraced, the Truth. He was prepared. He had studied. He knew all the arguments against it! And all the answers for it!

Ananias led him to the courtyard where the servants were preparing breakfast. "First you must eat and regain your strength. This will not be easy. There are many who want to destroy The Way." Ananias stopped speaking suddenly and covered his mouth with his hands, realizing what he had just said.

Saul bowed his head in shame. "I know, Ananias. I was one of them. But if I can be persuaded, maybe they can also be convinced. I will try—no matter what the cost."

After Ananias bid him goodbye, assuring him he would be back to introduce him to other believers, Saul slowly walked through the courtyard and into a garden bordering Judas' property. The garden was quiet—flowers of many varieties providing a fragrant smell that was calming. Saul looked up for a moment and saw in the middle of the garden a great, gnarled olive tree. Memories of a dark-haired young girl stole unbidden into his mind. As tears rolled down his cheeks unnoticed, Saul knelt close to the olive tree and prayed for forgiveness. He spoke to Abigail as if she was there with him, nestled among the roots of the tree. He spoke to his son and to his unborn child. "You tried to lead me to the light and I tossed you aside. Now you are with the Light and I will do everything I can to meet you there someday. Shalom, my loved ones. Shalom." He felt a breeze toss his hair, just the way his wife used to do with her hands in their most intimate times together.

Finally at peace, Saul brushed the dirt from his tunic and rose, placing a flower at the foot of the olive tree for Abigail.

Printed in the United States
33652LVS00002B/88-111